ASUNDER

Marie's job as a museum guard at the National Gallery in London offers her the life she always wanted, one of invisibility and quiet contemplation. But amid the hushed corridors of the Gallery lingers the legacy of her great-grandfather Ted, the warder who slipped and fell moments before reaching the suffragette Mary Richardson as she took a blade to one of the Gallery's masterpieces on the eve of the First World War. After nine years, Marie begins to feel the tug of restlessness. A decisive change comes in the form of a winter trip to Paris — where her carefully contained world is suddenly torn apart . . .

LAMBERT

Smith

res   s.

• ye

• at

• nd gy,

• ıp,

RAMSBOTTOM
Please return/renew this item
by the last date shown.
Books may also be renewed by
phone or the Internet.

• rn

• yal

www.bury.gov.uk/libraries

Yo   n

Every contribution is gratefully received. If you
would like to help support the Foundation or
require further information, please contact:

THE ULVERSCROFT FOUNDATION
The Green, Bradgate Road, Anstey
Leicester LE7 7FU, England
Tel: (0116) 236 4325

website: www.foundation.ulverscroft.com

Chloe Aridjis was born in New York and grew up in the Netherlands and Mexico City. She received her DPhil in nineteenth-century French poetry and magic from Oxford, then lived in Berlin for five years. She currently lives in London.

CHLOE ARIDJIS

◆

ASUNDER

Complete and Unabridged

ULVERSCROFT
Leicester

First published in Great Britain in 2013 by
Chatto & Windus
London

First Large Print Edition
published 2014
by arrangement with
The Random House Group Limited
London

A catalogue record for this book is available
from the British Library.

ISBN 978–1–4448–1926–7

Published by
F. A. Thorpe (Publishing)
Anstey, Leicestershire

Set by Words & Graphics Ltd.
Anstey, Leicestershire
Printed and bound in Great Britain by
T. J. International Ltd., Padstow, Cornwall

This book is printed on acid-free paper

*If one hundred dogs bark at a phantom,
the phantom becomes reality.*

1

They call us guards, warders, invigilators, room keepers, gallery assistants. We are watchmen, sentinels, but we don't polish guns, shoes or egos. We are custodians of a national treasure, a treasure beyond value stored behind eight Corinthian columns of a neoclassical façade, the dreams of the ancients stuccoed to our building. And our title should honour that.

I came to my profession half by chance, half following an ancestral call. After stumbling upon an ad for a Travelling Exhibition Assistant, I applied for the position but found the vacancy had been filled. Yet the kind man who answered my call mentioned another opening, this one at the British Museum. A guard had just resigned due to the diagnosis of an incurable ailment, and decided he wanted to spend his remaining months staring at something other than nymphs and satyrs locked in battle. They offered him the choice of other wings but he said he wanted to leave London and retire from culture.

My time there didn't last but it led me to

my calling. After the British Museum came the National Gallery, and nine years later I have come to know all the paintings and panels better than the palm of my hand.

How will you handle the boredom, they had first asked at the job interview. I laughed before realising they were serious, and told them I didn't easily grow bored. But you will, they warned, and I replied that I would then simply draw up lists in my head or count the number of skirts or stripes in the room. You're meant to protect the works of art, they said, to which I replied of course, yes, I would.

Acedia plagues the novice much more than the experienced solitary; unlike some of the new guards, I do not suffer from boredom or listlessness. Half of us have the right temperament, the other half don't. Only time can distinguish us. Yet museum acedia isn't triggered by a crisis of faith or the shifting angle of the sun and, what's more, my profession is actually suited to those afflicted by it, perfect for individuals who are unconcerned with their position in the world and have fallen prey to a relatively permanent mental or physical sloth. The museum provides an activity for which we are paid to do little more than stand or sit for hours contemplating immobile images and mobile figures.

Occasionally I remind myself that I could have become a dozen things in life. I could have finished university, got a degree in English, perhaps added some letters after my name. I could have had a desk and a fountain pen, people knocking at the door bringing in papers to sign. Or, at the very least, my own filing cabinet and phone extension. But I have always been more interested in being than becoming, and as soon as I stumbled upon this job I knew nothing would budge me. Ambition has never been high on the list, nor marriage or adventure: the only thing that occasionally tempts me is the thought of another museum.

*　*　*

And I admit that at first I was more than a little jealous of the guards at Tate Modern, watching over their collection housed within an old power station, yet the energy being generated, while neither nuclear nor electric, came with its own set of perils. But it wasn't until the Scandinavian artist set up an immense fake sun in the Turbine Hall that I thanked my guardian angels for my job at the National Gallery.

Until then, it is true, I envied my colleagues

at the new Tate, and when this sun first rose I would, on days off, walk along the river to the museum and spend long whiles on my back staring upwards. A mirror had been fastened to the ceiling and there'd be dozens of us lying in random configurations on the concrete floor, waving at our reflections above, and I felt like I was at a site of pagan worship, all eyes converging on this great yellow sphere whose emanations remained a mystery — that is, until the guards began complaining of headaches and dizziness and cursing the fumes released from the artificial astral body, especially Martin Strake who, already prone to migraines and sensitivity to light, made a point from the start of looking the other way. After a few weeks the monofrequency lamps really took their toll; Martin succumbed to their haze, his legs grew weaker, his eyesight began to blur, his movements trance-like as if dictated by this overhead sun, attached to it by invisible strings.

And I succumbed, I too, and for several weeks went to worship the ephemeral god, until I found out this supposed orb wasn't even a whole but a semicircle. We had been going to pay our respects to a semicircle, made whole by its reflection in a mirror. To this day I wish I hadn't looked at the

4

catalogue and had continued with my fantasy of the whole, but in the end, all that matters is that the Scandinavian's piece was eventually replaced by something else of monstrous proportions yet not as precarious and that Martin Strake gradually regained his former self and could turn his eyes towards the Turbine Hall without dissolving. I used to envy those who were assigned temporary rather than permanent exhibits before realising that temporary is too risky; you never know what you are going to get.

*　*　*

Life at our Gallery is more predictable.

Early each week we are assigned different sections of a wing and, within these sections, four rooms a day. In the morning we shed our civvy clothes and slip on our uniform: a mouse-grey jacket with matching trousers or skirt, a pale lilac shirt and a shiny purple tie. We are given twenty-four minutes a day to change, an iron always available in the changing room, and in my nine years working here those twelve minutes in the morning and twelve in the evening, during which all kinds of little transformations take place, have gone by in a flash.

Once the museum opens at ten we must be

in uniform and at our post. As of that moment we start patrolling our rooms, followed by a forty-five-minute lunch break, then back to our rooms. We have two twenty-minute tea breaks, morning and afternoon. It works well, this variation, after a while even beauty grows tiresome, and I have served every room in the Gallery except for the Portico Patrol, for which special training and a more assertive temperament, ideally, are required. Rotation is the salvation of the museum guard.

★　★　★

Our job has often been regarded as a knacker's yard, the final outpost at the end of a long journey. Many of my colleagues are in their fifties and sixties, a few even older. People usually end up here after working in something else for years. George used to sort letters at the head post office at Mount Pleasant from midnight to four in the morning. Charlie worked as a car mechanic at his brother's garage in Clapton. Pat began the job only after the last of her six children had left home. John was a nightwatchman at a bank for three decades. Dave spent twenty-eight years tweaking rides at the carny. Janet had gone bankrupt and was forced to sell her pub. Roland worked at a construction company called Sisyphus until suffering a nervous breakdown caused by a speed habit and industrial fatigue.

Some of us live in Zone 1 or 2, others in Zone 3 or 4 and spend an hour on public transport each morning. Some of us have a degree, most of us don't. Some of us look at the art, some of us don't. But we all protect the pictures and are able to direct visitors towards an entrance, an exit, towards whatever they want to aim for or depart from.

In the canteen, during one of the many hypothetical conversations we liked to engage in, conversations that led nowhere and for that very reason were all the more entertaining, we established that if most of us were given a painting we would sell it off immediately. Another hypothetical scenario is *Which painting would you save if there were a fire*. Some colleagues would choose a specific work they'd run to remove from the wall, others had none in mind, and yet others tried to think of the most valuable, usually a da Vinci or, for some reason, a Manet.

I was fond of my colleagues, every one of them, and welcomed the sight and sound of them most mornings, first my female colleagues in the changing rooms, where we'd often touch up our faces and comb the city from our hair, and then the male ones during team assembly, always taking note when Roland or another favourite was absent, which wasn't often, given the serious nature of our job.

★ ★ ★

It was nearing four that Tuesday, an autumn day that had started like any other, and the light in the museum lay on the cusp of natural and artificial illumination, the sky-lights and louvres still filtering in what they could of the early dusk, the light sensors poised to climb a notch as soon as they registered a gloaming.

I was in Room 25 with the van Hoogstraten peepshow, always a source of curiosity, at least at first. Four adolescents came in and gathered round, taking turns to peer in through the side holes as if they were dark forbidden slits. Yet I knew their interest wouldn't last. Despite the cupids on the exterior, the Hoogstraten contained nothing but a masterly exercise in perspective: the bare, orderly, well-swept interior of a seventeenth-century Dutch home, the only living beings a spaniel with tawny eyes and two women, one nightcapped in bed and the other seated in the far background reading a book, with the silhouette of a man behind a door.

Familiar with expressions of disappointment, the promise of something erotic trumped by the everyday, I watched with satisfaction as the teenagers shrugged and moved on.

And then I saw the man's face heading towards me, his short legs taking long strides in my direction, and though his command of English was shaky he managed to articulate with a few words and as many gestures that he and his wife had noticed that the guard in Room 23 was unwell.

I left the teenagers and hurried to tell Roland, who was haunting the threshold between 26 and 27, that I was going to investigate an incident and could he in the meantime alert Security, and with that I took a sharp turn into Room 23 to find my colleague Leighton Crooke slouched in his black leather chair. Instead of the formal vertical required of our profession, his body was slanting to the right, a forty-degree angle tipping into forty-five, as if nailed to the chair at the base but struggling, after decades of obedience, to wrench itself free. His eyes had withdrawn their vigil and his hands lay formless and inert in his lap. I approached as calmly as I could and tapped the stiff shoulder encased in the grey uniform. Crooke was nearly seventy and had dozed off on the job before.

After the tapping failed to produce a reaction I held up his wrist and felt for his pulse, pressing lightly and then, upon feeling nothing, a bit harder. It seemed extremely faint, if present at all, but I didn't trust myself to declare any man dead or alive — I thought I could detect some faint life current but wasn't sure, it could simply be the residual warmth of an expired system — and, fearing it would soon be altogether nonexistent, I stepped out of the way to allow Frances from Human Resources to take charge. With a cool air of authority, years of moving with ease through the different strata of our museum, she crouched down beside Crooke and reached for his other wrist, removed his watch, and pressed her forefinger and middle finger against the base of his thumb far more assertively than I had, the pale blue veins that ran beneath his papery skin forming an unlikely continuum with the blood-red polish of her nails.

Curious visitors had begun to turn away from the pictures towards the spectacle in the chair, and I could almost sense the man's fading pulse radiating outwards into the room as if searching to latch onto new hosts.

Two more colleagues arrived, murmuring loudly, their agitation unconcealed. Frances stood up, straightened her skirt and asked us to help clear the room. Just as the last visitors, the couple who'd found him, by then probably feeling invested in the man's fate, had left, four medics rushed in through the far door with a stretcher.

Something was happening in the Gallery, a flicker of an event that would be committed to the annals, and this time I was part of it, though from a historical perspective it was only the quiet death of a sixty-eight-year-old felled, most likely, by a heart attack, I had to remind myself as I watched sadly on as the corpse was gently lifted, laid out on the stretcher, and removed.

2

The dusk of Millbank had filled with the amber lozenges of unoccupied black cabs, miners with lantern-strapped foreheads rushing towards or away from the city centre, as I made my way to meet Daniel at the Drunken Duck, a pub a few streets from Tate Britain.

I stepped inside and searched for my friend in the noisy crowd that had gathered amidst the wooden stools and nodding taps, and eventually found him at a table that offered a strategic view of his current passion. The girl at the bar, though he had yet to speak to her.

'I'm sorry about Crooke,' were his first words once I'd removed my coat and draped it over a chair. 'I remember him from my years there . . . He seemed like a good man.'

'Yes, I thought so too. How did you hear?'

'Oh, the news reached us pretty quickly,' he said, pushing a pint of beer towards me. 'I got stout, hope that's okay.'

'Thank you,' I said, though he knew I preferred wine.

He shot a longing look in the direction of the bar, then turned back to me, his heavy-lidded blue eyes sloping down into his temples with the melancholy that sometimes crept into his face when he wanted something he couldn't have.

★ ★ ★

Daniel Harper and I met nine years ago, patrolling neighbouring rooms of the Sainsbury Wing and, by day four or five, discovered a kinship. His air was removed, fugitive and self-contained, his focus on something far beyond the Gallery's grand portico and vestibules, and from the start he struck me as different from the other guards. Whenever I'd peer into the next room I'd see him either pacing back and forth or writing in a notebook. He wrote at lightning speed, I observed, yet when visitors entered the room the notebook would vanish into his pocket like a magic trick in reverse. I couldn't figure out what he was writing — cricket scores, shopping lists, endless games of noughts and crosses — but he did it with such stealth, I imagined it must be something confidential; I later found out they were poems.

Apart from his withdrawn aura, the other noteworthy characteristic was his limp, a visual stutter that accompanied most of his movements. When stationary, he looked geometrically even; the moment he moved,

13

the evenness was lost.

Daniel was as honest, knowledgeable and courteous a guard as they come but in the end he was fired, fired for his pacing, since he couldn't keep still and would pace from one end of the room to the other, the pacing made worse by his limp, for he would take one step forward and then drag the other foot in its wake at four- to five-second intervals like a broken metronome. It didn't help when he changed to soft-soled orthopaedic shoes; you could still hear every step and drag of his feet. He would only come to rest when asked a question, but the moment he finished answering he would resume his tortuous path.

Because of his kindness and because, apart from the pacing, he was an exemplary guard who knew more about art than the rest of us, no one had the heart to complain, until one day a professor of early Flemish painting came to the Gallery to examine a triptych and by day six he was driven mad by the four- to five-second intervals and marched over to the management and lodged a complaint. It turns out this professor of early Flemish painting was married to one of the gallery's main patrons, Lady So-and-so, and one week later Daniel received a letter of dismissal. Nearly catatonic with disbelief, he stopped writing for a year, talking only about his 'pacing dragon', and how these two feet of his, pacing and dragging in close alliance, would spell the end of him.

* * *

A few months after his disappointment at the National Gallery, Daniel was offered a similar job at Tate Britain. The paintings weren't as magnificent, even the best of them, but he liked most of them too. The museum lay farther from home, now a bus and two Tube journeys rather than a simple bus ride, but he could use the time to read. And the building wasn't as large or grand as our Gallery, but at least it too was classical in style, with a six-column portico and a central dome. A different kind of cathedral, less holy and with fewer pilgrims, yet my friend was determined to protect the paintings with the same degree of devotion.

As for the other warders, they were of a different breed from those he was used to. He was amazed by how scarce they were and by how many rooms seemed to go without protection, but then realised there were fewer visitors as well. And unlike many of us at the Gallery, the guards at Tate Britain were mostly art students or aspiring artists who had no intention of spending their lives working in security.

At first Daniel had a crisis over the presence of so much twentieth-century, even contemporary, art — how could it compare, how could it coexist, with that of the past? He couldn't help feeling that by placing the centuries so close together they were stretching things, diluting the force of the greats, and it took him several weeks to stop feeling a jolt each time he turned from a room with Blakes or Turners into one containing less transcendent work.

Yet to enter the room with Turner's late paintings, he would say, was extraordinary, and made it all worthwhile, it was like entering a room of light, pure sunlight pouring forth from the walls, that was when the voltage surged, when the museum became a cathedral.

In fact, early on in our friendship we had agreed, during one of our very first conversations, that we much preferred the old to the new. It was far better to watch over art that had withstood the test of time — why devote hours of your life guarding something that might be gathering dust or mould in a warehouse fifty years from now?

★ ★ ★

'If the foreign couple hadn't noticed Crooke in his chair I would've probably been the one to discover him,' I reflected, 'when I'd moved on to Room 23.'

'We're thin lines of defence,' Daniel replied, tapping on his glass with two fingers.

'That we are,' I said, half relishing the thought.

Over the decades the museum lore gathered, mainly things overheard rather than witnessed first-hand. Among these were the widely circulated stories that had become public domain, such as the heavily lipsticked woman who kissed a white painting in order to cheer it up, and the guard at the Louvre who went around carving Xs into paintings with his own set of keys. And of course Rembrandt's *Night Watch*, attacked no less than three times in the past century. We came to hear about all sorts of museum pathologies, mostly involving people suffering from an identity crisis, paintings mistaken for mirrors as individuals caught sight of a troubling reflection.

At work we had been taught to be good judges of character, programmed to pick up on the slightest stirrings of unrest, to read faces and gauge their intentions. After so many years at the job, I had become finely skilled in the interpretation of a clenched fist, a skittish glance, the roaming gaze of someone unharnessed. I would try to detect whether there was something in immediate need of release, on the verge of eruption, a dangerous failure to distinguish one's personal life from that of a painting.

Daniel knew many more stories than I did, and additional ones from overseas, such as the irritable old ladies at the Hermitage who despite seeming languid and inert were in possession of sharp eyes and tongues, the mentally impaired guards at one of Munich's painting collections, and the custodians at Pompeii who flicked ash from their cigarettes into the ruins.

After he'd brought up some of these details yet again that evening, reminding me of the great yet for the most part untapped range of variables in our profession, I returned the conversation to poor Leighton Crooke, whose fading pulse I could still feel between my fingers, but as I spoke I could see Daniel's attention beginning to drift.

The girl at the bar was calling out — with a rather pronounced lisp that didn't match her looks — to a man who was walking away without collecting his change. But for a few degrees her face was nearly turned in our direction. Daniel made himself taller in his chair, straining to enter her line of vision.

Most of the time, like me, he did not care to draw notice to himself and was similarly content to carry out life at low volume. There was an abundance of loud people in the world, we agreed, and someone had to compensate, bring the dial down halfway. We preferred to stand back, cross our arms, and observe. The world was full of people rushing around trying to change things or make themselves seen. So it fell to the rest of us to withdraw from the foreground, just like those distant bluish landscapes in old paintings, so discreet you only notice them later. I liked to imagine our kind as thinkers in training, a flow of indefinite blue that deepens over time.

Ships in bottles steered by one tiny captain, Daniel liked to say. He too enjoyed the invisibility, of having gazes wash over him with indifference. But there at the pub that night he was desperate to have his presence acknowledged.

★　★　★

His first glimpse of her had been a profile, as she'd held a goblet to the tap of Leffe and waited for it to fill, and he'd stood at the bar transfixed, longing to see up close the face within the bob, the kind of cut-glass bob that in silent films framed a whole catalogue of faces. A new employee, he assumed, or the publican's daughter home from somewhere. He had never seen her before.

'She kind of looks like you but with a wonky eye,' he'd later said, and I remember being half flattered, half aghast, at the thought of looking like anyone or anyone looking like me, yet was intrigued by the wandering eye Daniel mentioned, wired up to its own puppeteer. From where I was sitting I could see there was indeed a resemblance, and when he returned, emboldened, to the bar for another round, he commented on her jagged black fringe, like that of a cabaret singer whose hair had been trimmed in the dark.

'Kind of like yours,' he'd added, with which again I had to agree, though I had my flatmate Jane to thank for that; she was the one in charge of trimming my fringe and also did it in the dark, in the darkness of self-absorption.

* * *

Daniel and I each had our collections, private and public, and beyond their horizons all we required was one solid friend. Neither of us had anyone else of significance in our lives, though every now and then he would fall prey to an obsession, for the most part unrequited, and I would have a brief encounter, usually with someone I dimly knew from my past, that didn't threaten the peace.

After meeting, ours had quickly settled into a friendship with thankfully little ambiguity, and though I was drawn to his face and found myself studying it from different angles, even having faintly erotic dreams about him once or twice a year, I could never imagine getting close.

At thirty-three my romantic past was far from populated — a modest list of names with few pangs attached, perhaps one or two vague regrets but certainly no one for whom I longed to rewind time. As for Daniel, he'd been married in his early twenties to a Japanese nurse, and the only lasting result of those three years, he said, was a twenty-eight-line poem, 'False Door to the Tomb'. He still occasionally dreamt of finding someone but over time had started to feel like the last remaining individual of a species, he said, a highly evolved bird with a highly evolved cry, his song unheard since he never shared it with anyone, and he'd even started to wonder whether perhaps the right female for him had become extinct, preceding him by days, decades or centuries; anything was possible, a tragic error in chronology or biodiversity.

The hours passed. I fetched the next round, and the next, Daniel having decided to continue his contemplation from afar. The girl was pretty, I conceded, with wide-set eyes that focused on different corners of the pub, and she had an aura of the past that tends to cast a spell over nostalgic types.

Dispensing with our plans for an early night, we ordered a snack from the blackboard and settled further into the clamour of that Tuesday evening, Daniel's attention looping in and out, and my own returning frequently to events in the Gallery that day.

A bell sounded through the pub. Last orders.

'Go on,' I urged him, 'she's just a girl with a jagged fringe and a wayward eye.'

But Daniel remained seated and when we got up to leave he shot one unreturned glance in her direction and followed me out; he knew as well as I, if not better, the danger of closing the distance even a fraction.

★ ★ ★

At night I prefer to take the bus home though it often means transferring. To descend into the brightness of the Tube cancels out the day's end too brusquely, while buses do the opposite by carrying you through the pensive streets. I found a seat towards the back and settled in by the window, preparing myself for a quiet journey.

A masculine woman smelling strongly of roast coffee came to sit beside me. I tried to relax, the smell was quite pleasant, but the driver turned out to be extremely erratic, stepping on the accelerator at odd moments, lurching forwards along with the traffic, bolting the moment a clear strip opened up, each jerk knocking me against the passenger by my side, who didn't react. As we zoomed past bags of rubbish awaiting dawn collection, yesterday's debris ready to be carted off to make room for tomorrow's, I thought about Leighton Crooke and how quickly he'd been removed from his chair at the Gallery. I'd sometimes watched him in the canteen, the museum juncture that best offered a glimpse into the lives of colleagues, not the most exciting glimpse but one nonetheless. Some individuals brought their own lunch, prepared by a spouse or themselves, the distinction apparent in the detail, others purchased hot food at the counter. Leighton Crooke always bought his food there at the counter, never anything from home as far as I could tell, and occasionally our trays would end up face to face. The widower was given to mood swings; sometimes he would talk about everything from rising bus fares to the proliferation of shopping bags in his kitchen cabinet, at others he would clunk himself down with a sullen expression and not extend more than a nod in my direction.

Like some of our more frequent visitors, a handful of individuals who'd come in regularly to look at people, not paintings, I sensed that Crooke found an escape from solitude in our museum, drawn to the airy space and soothed by its ebb and flow.

Roland too loved the ebb and flow, or so he claimed, Roland the former speed freak in search of stillness. He was proud of his new set of teeth, years of savings turned to enamel, and after speaking he'd clench his jaw to make sure nothing had come loose. His real teeth had gone years ago, first to grinding and then to rot, but now he was calm, as if the accelerator had been removed from his system. Once Daniel left the Gallery he quickly became my favourite colleague, and certainly the most handsome, with a face that looked more painted than real. As he stood between rooms, tall and creaky like an old wooden puppet, I'd scarcely notice he was in uniform.

The 38 bus deposited me steps away from
where Essex Road joins Cross Street, the stop
and short route home so familiar I could
trace them in my sleep, though I'd be loath to
miss my nightly dose of Get Stuffed, the
taxidermy shop on the corner. It was always
closed — visitors by appointment only — yet
through the rhombus-shaped grille, which
broke up the already bizarre view into
kaleidoscopic fragments, I would peer in to
see a pricked ear, a snout, a stripe or a raised
paw, and the lifeless tails, now little more
than stopped markers of time.

Whenever I looked in my gaze would land
on something disquieting, whether the two
mounted zebra heads or the dangling bat with
outstretched wings or the mother kangaroo
with the motionless baby in her pouch. At
night the shop would remain lit up, the only
concession the owner made between his
animals and the outside world. That evening I
cast a sidelong glance as I walked past, then
stopped and did a double take. For a few
seconds I was certain I saw Leighton
Crooke's figure there at the back, stuffed and
inert and sitting upright, but when I looked
again I realised it was only the imprint left by
the owner, a man with raccoon-ringed eyes

whom I'd often see in the morning hunched over his desk at the far end, an uninviting silhouette surrounded by his menagerie.

★ ★ ★

I ran into my flatmate as soon as I walked through the door. She had either just arrived or been waiting impatiently for my return.

'Have you been at the moths again?' she asked, her lips and teeth stained red with wine. Jane worked as a scout and publicist at Hunchback Records, a small independent label; her evenings were filled with gigs and record release parties and she was rarely home before one. That night she was back early.

I removed my coat and shook my hair out from under my hat.

'One of the strips in the living room's missing.'

'I may have borrowed it.'

'You're meant to replace them.'

'I was going to, this weekend.'

'Well, in the meantime who knows how many moths will get at my clothes.'

'Jane, it's November.'

'You know every season is moth season here.'

She was right. We had them all year round.

'I'll buy you a couple of new ones tomorrow.'

'Have you taken any others?'

'No, I only needed one for now.'

* * *

Jane's bedroom was divided in half by two clothes racks from which her shirts and dresses hung colour-coordinated, black items at one end slowly conceding to colour, and in the middle of each rack was an adhesive white strip on which constellations of little brown moths had met their fate. At least once a day she would check these strips, counting to see whether there were any additions, moths angled skywards, tiny papery aeroplanes grounded at take-off, their antennae raised, bodies glued flat. She had also laid out strips in the living room and kitchen; for my own reasons, I would check on them too.

I promised I would replace it the following day.

Satisfied with my answer, she turned towards her room, but before leaving asked whether I'd like to accompany her to Camden the following Sunday to buy a corset. Despite having made a point, for years, of not returning to Camden, I said yes.

I'd tell her about my semi-eventful day another time.

I crossed our small living room and closed the window Jane had left open, shutting out the traffic sounds. Our flat lay on the noisy Essex Road, directly above the Sea Dragon aquarium, whose Chinese owner, purveyor of cold water, marine and tropical fish, would spend his days in the entrance of his shop with his arms crossed. As far as I could tell this was his only activity, to gaze longingly across the street at the successful fishmonger Steve Hatt, purveyor of dead and for the most part monochrome fish with splashes of pink and silver, his merchandise infinitely more in demand than the living harlequin kind. We never went to either place; the closer you live to a shop, the less likely you are to enter.

In my room I headed straight to the shelf on the wall, to the right of my bed, and stopped. From one collection to the other, that was the way, and only very occasionally did I feel like prying open a space between the two in that nebulous area called real life. There they lay, my eighteen miniature landscapes, in their current semi-random order, their slopes and plateaus rammed into smaller dimensions, their geological memory handed to them all at once. I picked up an eggshell and tilted it towards the light, admiring the autumn landscape that would never meet winter, fiery leaves the size of rice grains forever fastened to mini branches, the painted gold sky unsilenced by any solstice or atmospheric disturbance. This autumn eggshell was the first I'd crafted, before making spring, and, months later, winter and summer, always indifferent to the real season at hand.

I'd then fashioned a mountain, coated with real soil and faded grass, its peak a powdery white, a moth glued halfway up its steep face in perpetual ascent. And then warmer scenarios. A volcano with its upper and lower mantle, marbled crust and chamber of magma. A desertscape that lay somewhere outside time, its pinkish sand in permanent undulation.

Two seascapes: choppy waves of crystallised sugar, boats with slanted masts and torn sails of gauze. For the dark clouds pressing down on the horizon I'd rubbed cigarette ash onto tufts of cotton and flecked the borders with ink, then suspended them with nearly invisible threads. Skies hooked up to backboards, seas tethered to a tiny plank.

All was possible, and nothing.

After a year or two of open landscapes on boards I turned my attention towards interiors. The first was a grotto in an eggshell, with a jagged tooth from my parents' old cat glued to the centre. Then, a cave with miniature wax stalactites and stalagmites inhabited by tiny liquorice bats. A pale blue eggshell with a small door gave on to an interior night sky, the stars dots of silver metallic marker on a background of Indian ink. A low Dutch horizon, with toothpick windmills, hinted at human presence and endeavour minus the actual humans to complicate matters.

★　★　★

No human figures. Only moths. The idea originated when I moved to Essex Road. First, from a sign in the window of Get Stuffed assuring customers that animals weren't ever sacrificed in the name of taxidermy and that many of the specimens such as foxes had come from roadkill — and then when I saw Jane and her moth strips. Yes, cruel, but at least I put the cruelty to use. So I added these stilled lives to my still lifes, and I liked the results. Let them die for something.

With my pair of little nail scissors I would cut round the outline of their bodies, the fatal strip serving as a ready mount. At first I'd tried to detach them but their wings would crumble between my fingers. Once I'd cut one out I would then paste it onto a desert, mountain, a ship at sea.

Over the months the moth would slowly, very gradually, decompose, coating everything in a fine brown sparkly powder, and then the time would come to check on the strips again, the pheromones having continued to issue their wicked siren call. I don't know what would happen were I to stop living with Jane, whether I would go out and buy them myself; it was simply part of the ecosystem within the flat.

⋆   ⋆   ⋆

The landscapes came naturally to me. From the start, it was as if a mysterious hand had taken hold of mine and directed it. Without the help of a manual I'd known where to cut an eggshell, in which direction to make the incision, how to gently detach a quarter or a half. First I'd make a hole at the top, tip the egg over and empty its final contents with a syringe. Once it was clean and dry I'd cut and fortify, with glued paper or varnish. At first I used the sharpest knife in the kitchen but after some research went out and bought myself an oblique burin, its steel blade slicing happily along the calibration lines I'd marked on the shell. I would carve through the centre halfway horizontally, then halfway vertically, and remove one of the upper quarters so that the bottom half remained, ready to welcome its features.

Emptied, strengthened, given a new horizon. A strip of blue paper, the sky. A strip of white, a coat of winter. A strip of green, an untrampled field. A square of black, a patch of night. I would insert mountains of cork, lakes of pressed aluminium foil, trees of cotton impaled on match-sticks. The stands for the eggshells were cardboard, little circular pedestals on which each oval was balanced.

By the end of each week a fine layer of dust would come to settle over everything, gathering more thickly in the gaps and ridges between topographical features, and I'd use a special cloth to remove it. This handmade collection of mine, eighteen and slowly growing, formed a nuclear centre into which everything fed back, and when I returned home from a day's work or an evening out I would head straight over. Time was collapsed into them, the smaller, the more infinite, and every now and then I'd hold up a magnifying glass to one to see whether over the years some secret message had surfaced but I never found anything, and of course magnification tends to dent fantasy rather than enlarge it.

Sometimes I would adjust one, inspired by a detail I'd noticed in a painting or else simply aligning things with my current mood, for I hated bucolic landscapes when I was feeling stormy, and stormy landscapes when I was feeling calm. I'd tear off a few leaves and scatter them on the ground, or loosen some sand in the desert, tiny acts of immense satisfaction.

That evening I held up the volcano, one of my favourites, noticing how much dust had collected in the crater and how the moth on its side would soon have to be replaced, since a bit of its wing was missing or, rather, had crumbled away. I reached for a tissue and carefully cleaned out the crater's mouth, the red paint intensifying almost immediately as if the volcano itself were becoming active.

3

Mornings when I'd emerge from Green Park Tube and into the thrum of Piccadilly towards Trafalgar Square I would often pause outside Fortnum & Mason with my coffee and stare at the lavish window displays, imagining the symphony with which the glass panes would shatter and splinter into a thousand tiny shards littering the pavement with fractured light, the same shop windows into which my great-grandfather Ted would've gazed decades and decades before, when he too was a warder at the National Gallery.

I considered myself fortunate to be connected via my lineage to one of the most significant incidents in our museum. Nothing could rival the story Ted had experienced first-hand, and over the decades the details, reviewed a thousand times in my mind, grew so familiar they almost became my own.

★ ★ ★

Until the last days of his life he could remember what he'd eaten for breakfast that

34

morning of 10 March 1914, and the southerly wind that blew into London as he kissed my great-grandmother goodbye and set out for work. Yet Ted wasn't the only one making his way towards the National Gallery at half past nine. As he travelled down Piccadilly a small woman in grey was taking the back streets, crossing Soho at a brisk pace, scarcely aware of the shops awakening around her, bisecting Leicester Square in a hurried diagonal. Small in size and fitted neatly into her skirt and coat, she cut a figure so demure that people would scarcely have noticed her.

Upon reaching Trafalgar Square she slowed her steps and entered the National Gallery through the main door like everyone else. Entry was free on Tuesdays yet it was still early, a few minutes past ten, and visitors had only just started to trickle in. She toured the rooms, taking in the familiar paintings, paused in Room 17, lingered elsewhere with her sketchbook.

Noon drew closer. People started heading out for lunch. The woman in grey returned to Room 17 and walked slowly over towards Velázquez's Rokeby Venus, which hung on the north wall on the right-hand side. Purchased for £45,000 by public subscription eight years earlier, the painting drew large numbers of visitors and was the artist's only surviving nude. On the plush seat in front of her, two large men with broad shoulders sat staring ahead.

The woman started to sketch. One of the men rose from his seat and wandered out. The other crossed his legs and raised a newspaper to his face. This very paper, across whose front page her name would be emblazoned the following day, conveniently hid her from view.

The first blow shattered the thick protective panel. She was experienced in the shattering of glass, mostly in the way of shop windows, but marvelled at how easily it yielded. The plate, one third of an inch thick, cracked in all directions. At first, the seated man — a detective assigned, with his colleague, precisely because of the suffragette threat — thought it was the skylight, which was being repaired that morning, and rushed to where a ladder had been left propped against the wall. From the opposite end of the room a warder, alerted to the drama at hand, started to rush over but slipped on the polished wooden floor and, as is often the way in history, this slowed him down for a few critical seconds.

The next six or seven blows were to the canvas itself. With her meat cleaver the young woman started at the nape of Venus's neck, then onto the spot between her creamy white shoulders, then downwards, aiming wherever her wrist felt pulled. She kept plunging and plunging, continually amazed at the efficiency of this small instrument she had bought with her last shillings at the ironmonger's on Theobald's Road. Fastened inside her sleeve with a chain of safety pins, a light tap to the last pin was all it had taken to release it.

Two Baedekers, perfectly aimed, came crashing against her own nape. She turned and saw two angry German tourists. People came at her from all directions. Hands grabbed her, dragged her, pulled and held her down. The floor was covered in fragments of glass. But it was too late. With her cleaver she had attacked flesh far more treasured than any slab of meat, and that was the point, she later said, to destroy the most beautiful woman in mythology in order to protest the imprisonment of another 'beautiful' woman, Emmeline Pankhurst, a fellow suffragette.

The angry crowd became a confused heap. It tumbled out of the room, into the stairwell, down the stairs, creating pandemonium all around, while back in Room 17, immune to the commotion, a torn Venus continued to repose in her satin boudoir while Cupid held a mirror up to her tranquil face.

The account in *The Times* the next day was extravagantly anatomical: *a cruel wound in the neck, for three or four inches it runs almost vertically, and spreads out an inch wide; another severe cut aggravated apparently by the chopper's having been twisted a little as it withdrew for the next blow; a broad laceration starting near the left shoulder and roughly forming, with two or three cuts, the letter N; two of the limbs of that letter are six or eight inches long, and the third is a gash extending right beyond the body and some inches through the drapery below it; the other cuts are cleanly made in the region of the waist . . . downwards nothing remains of the glass except splintered fragments filling the base of the frame and spreading out in front . . .*

Each time Ted told the story I would listen enraptured as he described the way in which from one second to the next a small, nervous figure in grey, the grey of an overcast day, had morphed into an arrow of fury and begun hacking away at the nude woman on the wall. He had been the very warder assigned to Room 17 in those days before rotation.

Startled by the shattering glass and the frenzied movements of the detective, who until then had been sitting calmly with his newspaper, my great-grandfather had started to run over but slipped on the floor, which had just been assiduously polished, and, losing his balance, landed on his face, scarcely registering the fall as he scrambled back to his feet. For the rest of his life, he would ask himself what would have happened had he crossed those seven yards and reached the suffragette, whether he would have wrestled her to the floor and torn the cleaver from her furious hand, or whether he would have lost courage at the last minute or one of his fingers in the struggle. In the end, it was a collective effort that brought down the small woman and by the time he'd arrived a tumbleweed of fists, boots and curses had erupted around her.

Looking back, I don't know what side I would have been on. When Ted told me his stories I assumed there could only be one side. But I loved him just a tiny bit more for not having reached her in time.

★ ★ ★

Hours after the attack, the Board of Trustees held a special meeting in which it was decided that the Galleries, which had closed within minutes of the outrage, would remain shut for another two weeks. Further measures were discussed, then implemented: that not more than half the Exhibition Rooms in the main floor be opened on alternate days, that the staff be concentrated and increased, that the Treasury make allowances to employ a number of commissioners to in turn provide custodians to look after the rooms, that all visitors surrender muffs, stoles, bags, parcels, sticks and umbrellas at the stalls at the entrance, that the most important pictures in the Gallery be protected by thicker panes of glass, that the director order experimental barriers to be placed in certain rooms, that all students, before admission, make a solemn declaration not to wilfully injure the pictures.

Those were anxious days, Ted would say, anxious days in the museum. Warned against the pilferer and the crank, guards remained on the lookout for meat cleavers and umbrella sticks. Even before Mary Richardson — known as Polly Dick to those who loved her, Slasher Mary to those who didn't — Ted had been asked to keep an especially sharp watch on female visitors of all ages, especially those not accompanied by men. A year earlier, he and his colleagues had received copies of photographs of militant suffragettes taken by the government. Staff were asked to study these surveillance pictures and identify any of the women should they happen to enter the rooms.

Ted had kept one, a silver print mounted onto an identification sheet in the folder of Gallery documents he stowed in a drawer of his bedside table, and one day, on my fourteenth birthday, he showed it to me, only once, as if a longer exposure might hurt my eyes. I remember how struck I was by the eight black and white numbered portraits of for the most part attractive, proud-looking women, the angular cut of their jackets, the long skirts, the high collars, most with a pin or a tie fastened at the centre as if holding everything in place. Their hair seemed to be worn in three varieties: pulled tightly back, tucked into a hat, or else falling over their shoulders in tresses: sternness, modesty, abandon.

Taken largely unawares, the pictures showed the suffragettes between or shortly after performances, either being led away by the arm or else in a rare moment of repose, a gleam of disquiet in the eyes of the woman walking down the street, pausing at a corner with her parasol, touring the prison yard. They were such a far cry, these strange portraits, from the painted women at the Gallery, and though Ted only brought them out once their faces lodged themselves in my mind.

★ ★ ★

Madmen and hysterics are born into every generation, Ted would say, and though I knew he wasn't referring to me something inside would inevitably shudder, his words a coin dropped into a deep well whose bottom was reached only decades later. Remember, he'd say, appearances can be misleading, just look at the havoc wrought by this small woman in grey. At five feet five and a half inches, look at the scale of damage she inflicted on the large, magnificent painting, into which her entire frame would have fit . . . There's no telling . . .

Yet in the end, the Rokeby Venus hadn't cost much to repair, thanks to the supposed intervention of one aptly named Helmut Ruhemann, chief restorer at the Gallery, who almost certainly drew on a lot of patience and tranquillity, or *Rühe*, our German colleague Dieter once suggested, to carry out the task. Well, most say it was Ruhemann who restored Venus to her previous state but my great-grandfather always insisted it was one Horace Buttery, a highly respected restorer of paintings from collections in London, Oxford, Cambridge and beyond, who did the actual work. Just how, Ted wanted to know in his final years, did the credit go to Ruhemann, who, as far as he understood, had merely cleaned the Rokeby

Venus rather than restored her.

Whatever the truth, Helmut Ruhemann, native of Berlin and later of various addresses in North London, was, in the eyes of museum directors, one of the great immigrant restorers of the time. Unlike most of his contemporaries, he boldly advocated the complete removal of varnish in the cleaning of paintings, of which he limited himself to European easels, and insisted that any attempt at leaving even a thin layer of the old varnish would nearly always fail, and prevent the painting's reawakening. Light has to pass twice through a varnish, he pointed out, on its way to the picture surface and then on its way back to the viewer, so the light-absorbing effect of a dark varnish is doubled.

A return to the original is what Ruhemann upheld, the removal of later layers of varnish, stripped away to the original tranquillity. The intention of the master should be the guiding standard, he said, not the desires of the general public, who might at first be dazed by the brightness of the canvas like someone who has lived too long in a darkened room.

★ ★ ★

As for Mary Richardson, Ted would say, there was no return to the original. After the attack

43

she was sent to Holloway Prison, home to many a suffragette, for six months, the longest possible sentence for damaging a work of art. She had already served time there for assaulting policemen, flinging an inkpot through the window of a police station, and breaking windows at the Colonial Office and Holloway.

When she was brought there on 10 March 1914 the medical advisor warned of appendicitis yet the administration took little heed. When she refused to eat she was forcibly fed, a medieval torture to which fasting suffragettes were subjected, and then released with appendicitis a month later in accordance with the Cat and Mouse Act, which declared hunger strikers be freed from prison until healthy enough for re-arrest. The special police Cats would wait outside their homes ready to pounce, Ted explained, while the Mice rested and strategised indoors. Mary Richardson was re-arrested and forcibly fed, then released again with appendicitis. The appendicitis became acute; her mouth scarred by the fingernails of prison officials. The longer she campaigned, the further away from tranquillity.

★ ★ ★

44

Velázquez established his legacy with brush-strokes, Mary Richardson with knife strokes, both with impassioned diagonals. I often searched for signs of the assault, how could I not, whenever I was assigned Room 30, which now held the painting. After staring for a minute or two, working my way from top to bottom and across the luminous flesh, I'd eventually find what looked like a fading bruise between Venus's shoulders resembling the faint imprint of a petrol stain, final remnants of a flammable spill from long ago.

★ ★ ★

As was often my way, I thought back on Ted that morning as I climbed the steps to the staff entrance of the Gallery, a cold, ancient gust blowing out of the building as I went in. I turned down the corridor to our changing rooms, stopping to glance at the plaque hanging in the foyer, an overdue gesture, added a little over a decade ago, honouring those colleagues who had died on duty. It was a rather modern plaque, a glass rectangle attached to the wall with four bolts, the names etched in black, and I couldn't help thinking that something more circular and brass-like would have been better. Since the plaque's appearance only five names had been chiselled in: a Mr Heeroo, Mr Chipperfield, Mr Szymanski, Mr Amin and Mr Lumsdale, the last in 2008, and I sometimes found myself secretly desiring an addition, as if time were slowing down a little too comfortably in our Gallery and needed a reminder of the cycles outside. Out of the five men listed I could only recall Mr Szymanski, an aged Pole with callused hands, extremely cordial with everyone but rather silent; his past and present were a mystery, his future easier to guess.

It took ten days for Leighton Crooke's name to be added. Once he passed away I checked at the end of the day too, just in case it'd appeared while the rest of us were upstairs patrolling. And so the five names chiselled into the glass grew to six, and each time I saw it I was reminded that I'd been witness to this small addendum to the museum archives. Yet after a while the event began to recede in our minds, drowned out by the louder tide of the Gallery.

4

During the final years of his life Ted would say that if something has vanished there's no need to remind yourself of its disappearance and if a place has changed there's no need to go and take measure. A memory has been shaped and slotted in your mind, found its plot among the others, why return as surveyor? Over the decades his London changed, within the museum and beyond, but he held on to the facts he knew.

I was in for a shock when I accompanied Jane to Camden the following Sunday. A chilly drizzle was falling as we emerged from the entrails of the Northern Line up into the grubby swirl round the station and then down the high street, swept up within seconds into the raggedy current heading towards the Lock.

One by one, I looked round and began adding up the losses. Gone was the shop where I used to buy late-night snacks and cigarettes. Gone was the café where I'd sit for hours watching local fauna come and go. Gone, worst of all, was Compendium, the marvel of a bookshop where I'd worked for eight months, my first job after dropping out of university. I'd heard of its demise years ago but had never visually acknowledged it until now. As we walked past the Doc Martens shop which had sprung up in its place, I recalled some of the anxiety I would experience there on a daily basis, the great worries over whether an important political theorist had gone astray and migrated to the comic books or whether a mathematician suddenly found himself amongst the Surrealists or a jazz musician in the Occult, details that meant everything at the time. As I superimposed a pyramid of books onto the jumble of shoes in the window display, I remembered the extremely kind and knowledgeable Scotsman who ran the fiction and poetry sections, and the way the owner would ask me if I'd read this writer or that, none of whom I had, but I got to know a few names and manifestos and more about politics than I ever did at university. I didn't put up a fight, however, when I was eventually replaced by a literature student who could direct customers to what they wanted with her eyes closed.

And then came the next jolt, Camden market itself. At first I wondered whether there'd been an error in geography but Jane assured me we had arrived at the Lock. It wasn't the Lock I recalled. As soon as we

48

entered I could see that here too familiar coordinates had been erased. Washed out to sea, the treasure troves selling music insignia; in their place, a surf of the tacky and tedious. And just to hammer in the sight of fluorescent T-shirts, spiky club wear and tribal body ornaments, the loud techno and drum & bass emerging from invisible speakers began to pound my temples. People kept bumping into me, changing direction every few seconds in a crisis of indecision, and I stuck as close as I could to Jane, who zigzagged through the market in pursuit of her corset.

Just as I was about to tell her I'd wait outside, I spotted a stall beyond the covered area, there on the periphery, and before even realising whose it was I grabbed Jane's sleeve and pulled her over. Something glittery had caught my eye, the pin of a scarab, its wings outspread in midflight, one of a dozen pins set in a black velvet board. Alongside this board was another, with silver rings in the shapes of skulls, bats, dragons and spiders.

The drizzle had stopped, the merchandise further polished by the fine drops, and after a quick survey Jane pulled down a thick black scarf that'd been hanging like a dead jackdaw from a pole overhead and I picked up the scarab, its little wings studded with fake diamonds sparkling as I turned it over in my hand.

'Beautiful, isn't it?'

A curl of smoke, a person within. From amidst the scarves and velvety boards emerged a slender figure with jet-black hair, high cheekbones and long lashes. Even without the make-up he was disarmingly handsome. Back in the day, every dame at the Bat Cave would have slept with him. Or had.

'Lucian,' I said.

He eyed me suspiciously, crushing a cigarette into the pewter face of a dragon, and reached for his pouch of tobacco.

'Marie?'

'Have I changed that much?'

He put down the tobacco and squinted, the cracks in his face deepening, and held out a large hand decked with rings. Within seconds it all came back: the strong grip, the enormous palm, the rings from Great Frog, that venerable institution in Ganton Street where he went for his own skull bibelots. Caricature or embodiment, I could no longer tell.

'And this is Jane,' I said.

'Jane,' Lucian repeated.

They shook hands, registered one another.

'How much is this scarab?' I asked.

'Twenty. You can have it for fifteen . . . So

how are you, Marie? You kind of disappeared. Just like that. Poof.' He snapped his fingers.

Seeing Lucian there in his skinny black jeans, Birthday Party T-shirt and studded belt wrapped twice round his waist set off vapours of memories. For two years we had shared a flat just off Camden High Street, a grim place but I wouldn't have wanted to live anywhere else at the time. It was his sole possession in the world, the fifty-six-metre-squared flat inherited from his grandmother, and he rented out the living room to make ends meet. He got the bedroom and I slept in our communal area on a mattress behind a screen. The kitchen had no stove, only a hotplate with two burners, but in those days we lived off pizza and curry. The bathroom was minute, with a shower like an upright coffin and tiles stained with black hair dye.

I'd like to say those were my shape-shifting days but the truth is, I didn't shift shape that often. Lucian, who was a good decade older, only invited me out with him a handful of times, on nights when he was feeling especially gallant or adrenalised. Yet looking back on those few nights, a crack of darkness between two eternities of light, I'd felt I was somebody, although the reality was, I went as his diluted shadow, always a few steps behind, stopping whenever he stopped to greet people, get drinks from the bar, light a cigarette, fix his hair, or whatever else required immediate attention.

Though they were few and far between, I vibrantly remembered those nights out. To the sound of his favourite tracks, he would prepare for hours as funereal voices mired in synthy graves or guitar riffs wafted out from under his bedroom door and circled the living room, following him to the bathroom as he stood at the mirror teasing his hair into an elaborate cobweb. Face, hair, nails, rings — white, black, black, silver: always in that order.

Once Lucian had donned his sooty threads and I'd put on my make-up and most alluring black clothes, usually a high-necked tunic or netted tanktop, we would jump on the bus to Soho. Occasionally we'd drop by the Intrepid Fox but usually we would head straight to Meard Street, home to the Bat Cave. Past the tattooed man at the door, from Soho into its netherho, I would follow Lucian as he embarked on his well-mapped journey through the insomniac rooms, past glow-worm faces in every nook and sequined Glams with trapeze-artist make-up who emitted sparkles each time they blinked their eyes, waved an arm or crossed their legs, past Goths huddled in corners like packed umbrella stands, every now and then unfolding their wings to dance to one of their anthems.

As we cut through the smoke of each room, billowing curtains parting just for us, Lucian would tip an imaginary hat towards nearly everyone he encountered. He was the Duke of the Bat Cave.

'And how much would this be?' Jane timidly held up the scarf.

'Ten for you,' Lucian said, staring down at her nails, which were painted a metallic greenish blue, a mermaid's tail or a drop of petrol.

'What's happened to Camden?' I asked. Before Camden, he'd sold bootlegs at Kensington Market, mostly of gigs he'd gone to himself, but once the place closed and with the days of bootlegs over, he had 'gone silver'.

Lucian glanced over at Jane before answering, then exhaled a large cloud of smoke.

'What's happened to our Camden. Bloody good question. It's a bloody nightmare. First the Emo kids and the cyber kids and the hippies began setting up, pushing us farther and farther out, and then there was that fire a few years ago. I knew we were finished. After that the developers were all over the place. Now it's just me and Black Rose and Elysium, those girls with the corsets and stuff, you remember Kate and Jackie, don't you? Tourists go to them when they come looking for Goth, but it all got a bit carnival if you know what I mean . . . I'm the last one here, and I don't think for much longer. Last year they moved me to this outside stall, where at least I can smoke, and knocked a hundred quid off the rent. I'm still holding on to the mast but with one hand . . . '

Jane shook her head in sympathy.

I asked about Louis.

'Still at the centre of your desk?'

'Dead centre.'

My first month in the flat, Lucian had spent half a year's savings on Louis, the skull of a twelve-year-old pickpocket trampled by a horse in 1852, or so the shop owner in Bloomsbury had claimed. Lucian placed him at the centre of his desk, right there between spilt tobacco and overflowing ashtrays, and Louis' eye sockets would watch as his owner rearranged rings on a board, strung silver bat wings into a bracelet, tightened the catch of a necklace. We always wondered what this little urchin had looked like, what his story had been. Perhaps he was the son of watercress sellers or chimney sweeps, lived in the slums of Bethnal Green or had recently come in from the provinces. Perhaps he'd moon-lighted as a mudlark, collecting debris fallen from boats on the river, a splash of the

Thames in his veins.

'And how are the ferrets?'

'Oh, my boys died long ago, didn't you know? They don't live forever.'

'I'm sorry to hear that.'

'Yeah, well, it's all origami shadows, isn't it?'

I nodded as if I understood.

Lucian's other great loves, apart from Louis, had been his two ferrets. They had the run of the flat and slept curled up in his armpits or, if he had a woman over, in a shallow hamper by the bed. Once they nearly drowned, when he took them to his friend Vince's and left the cage in the bathtub — it was only because one of them got up to use the bathroom that they discovered the ferrets' home floating in bathwater, their pointy ringed faces held just above the waterline. No one ever found out who'd turned on the tap since neither Lucian nor Vince had budged from the sofa where they'd been watching a film, and neither would have wished for that cruel burial at sea.

Conversation came to a standstill. Lucian looked at Jane again.

We said goodbye and started to walk away, back into the market's sacrificial heart.

'Marie,' Lucian called out, 'don't you want the pin?'

I returned to the stand and bought the little scarab. Jane didn't buy the scarf, however: an unspoken promise to return.

★   ★   ★

After Jane bought her corset at Elysium, so stirred up she didn't even bother trying it on and just held it up to her body for measure, we found the nearest exit from the market and were released. Questions and daydream all the way up the high street. She demanded to hear about Lucian. It's true I'd hardly mentioned him during my four years living with her, and certainly never in detail. Once that chapter in Camden, wedged between a flat share in King's Cross and our home in Essex Road, was over, I hadn't wanted to revisit.

★   ★   ★

It was a lifetime ago, at the end of a corridor past many shut doors, and I preferred to leave those doors shut and the corridor unlit.

Now I'd have to explain the longing that for two years often kept me awake behind my screen, the twitches of desire as I watched my handsome flatmate seduce everyone around, not to mention the few times I brought someone home myself, usually emotional boys from the bookshop or café, Lucian would stop speaking to me for days.

And once he began dating Sue, I knew I had to leave. Sue and Maxine, two tiger-eyed dames from the Bat Cave; once they appeared on the scene, the curtain fell. The cigaretted sisters we called them, or the Sisters of Mercy. They too had remained at the end of this corridor behind many shut doors, but now that I thought back on those days the image of them came quivering back in a waft of sulphur. Lucian had Sue, and his friend Perce got Maxine, at least on nights when Maxine felt like throwing someone a bone. They were two dark-haired beauties, candle white and always lit, one with her Dunhills and the other her Silk Cuts, and once they walked through the door I knew I could never compete.

So with Sue came the end of my life under the same roof as two ferrets, a Victorian pickpocket and a Camden Goth, and though Lucian could never understand why, he handled my decision to leave in an elegant way and even helped carry my two suitcases, books and hatbox down to the minicab waiting outside.

★　★　★

After witnessing the tiny flashes of desire between my former flatmate and my current one, new territory being tentatively marked out before my eyes, my only impulse — and a strong one — was to go and see Daniel. I rang and he was in, had finished writing for the day, and open to company. Jane and I said goodbye at the station. I watched her walk off clutching the plastic bag with her corset, mission accomplished though it seemed she might've just found the next one.

On the bus from Camden to Hackney, checking every now and then that the scarab was still affixed to my lapel, I thought back on the scene. For the first time in Jane's presence I'd felt like a shadow. At home she would be the one more likely to climb the walls or fall across a page, but there at the market it was I who lost substance. Even after all those years of not seeing Lucian he had, within minutes, sent me back to that insecure place, though at least I was no longer *his* shadow, maybe just a stray one, and solid enough anyway to carry a pin.

★ ★ ★

Daniel rented his flat in Hackney from two brothers who'd converted an old slipper factory into twenty spaces, either as work

58

units or as residential flats they let out to artists, DJs and graphic designers. Daniel didn't fall into any of these categories but with the help of a friend he was able to secure a good deal and had been living there for nearly six years. As luck would have it, the one and only vestige from the building's previous incarnation happened to be nailed to the floor of his living room: a peculiar medium-sized contraption with a wooden foot on which workers used to stretch or model slippers. The foot looked like that of a small adult, its heel attached to a pedestal on the machine and its smooth, toeless summit pointing towards the ceiling.

When I'd first gone over, I'd expected to stumble into an overgrowth of books, paper and objects, the sort of disorder within which I imagined every writer cocooned himself in order to write, yet when I arrived I was surprised to find austerity and restraint. Or maybe it was just laziness. No pictures on the walls, no objects on the shelves, no curtains on the windows apart from a large piece of cardboard he'd prop up at night. The furniture was sparse and mismatched, the only items with personality a long busy bookcase and a sagging maroon armchair where I'd deposit my things since the hooks by the door were taken up with dozens of scarves and coats he'd found at Oxfam.

Daniel buzzed me into the building and was waiting in the doorway of his flat when I reached the top of the stairs. He was in what he called his writing clothes, baggy cotton trousers and a blue T-shirt, his hair unevenly swept to one side, dark fronds falling onto his forehead. The familiar odour of coffee and pencil shavings hung in the air. After I'd tapped the slipper machine's wooden foot in a tiny concession to superstition and settled into the seat I always took by the window, he disappeared into the kitchen and came back out with tea and wine.

'How's your day been?' he asked, laying out mugs, pot and bottle.

'Just went to Camden with Jane and ran into Lucian.'

'Who?'

'Lucian. You remember, my old flatmate, the handsome Goth.'

'Oh yeah . . . And?'

'I guess it was nice to see him again. He's kind of unchanged. I think he really struck a chord in Jane.'

Daniel smiled. 'That makes sense.' He returned to the kitchen for wine glasses.

As I helped myself to the tea I realised I'd hardly eaten since breakfast. 'You wouldn't have anything small to eat, would you?'

'Not really. I need to do a big shop . . . But we can order in later.'

★ ★ ★

First, however, I knew I had to indulge the host, the rule whenever I went over. Before we spoke about our day or our week, before we ate or watched a film, Daniel would reach for a stack of letters, usually the most recent, and with the customary fervour read a few out to me. The only thing he would offer beforehand were liquids. And cigarettes, depending on whether I happened to be smoking at the time.

Along with his poems he had another collection — an ever growing, almost compulsive, correspondence with poets from around the world. One poet would introduce him to another, that one to another, and so on. Never by Internet, always by post: otherwise, the notion of country would mean so little. He had met only a handful of them, and preferred it that way. There were regular letters from a poet in Zagreb, from a Romanian translator in Stockholm named Pierre Zekeli, from someone in Rio de Janeiro. He knew little about their personal lives; many of these individuals, mostly men, were immensely shy, especially the Scandinavians. They would write frequently but get frantic should anyone but mention they were passing through their city. Then suddenly they were nowhere to be found, had to leave the country on urgent business, etc. But that suited him fine — with the few individuals he did meet, the correspondence suffered afterwards and in some cases even shrivelled up.

Inevitably, Daniel liked some of their work more than others'. But one should always be generous with one's colleagues, he would say, and he'd try to find something worthy in everything. The letters themselves were sometimes much more interesting than the poems. There was the German from Baden-Württemberg, for instance, who after learning that Daniel lived in a former slipper factory wrote to him about a fox on the wooded estate of a count who, over the course of two years, had amassed 300 pairs of shoes and slippers, predominantly leather slippers, since foxes, he explained, had a taste for leather and liked to sharpen their teeth on slippers in particular. This German poet had put out his own slippers one night when he went to stay at a nearby chalet, half hoping to be able to write himself into the story and, sure enough, in the morning his slippers had vanished.

Then there was the Austrian poet who suffered from lung disease, an ailment inseparable from his run-on sentences and never-ending paragraphs, as if each phrase were his last, a certain breathlessness in every letter, you could almost feel his lungs exerting themselves, Daniel said, trying to keep up with the velocity of his thought without losing momentum, and each time he received a missive from him he wondered whether it would be his last. Yet the letters kept coming.

The definition of the poet's solitude, Daniel would quote every now and then, is a circus number not announced in the programme.

Yet in my eyes he wasn't that alone.

Apart from the slipper machine, the flat's most intriguing item was an enormous nautilus shell so heavy I was never able to shift it a centimetre, and it was into the immense open ear of this shell, whose thick outer lip gave it the simultaneous appearance of a mouth, that Daniel read out his latest letters that evening. I poured myself some wine and tried to find a comfortable position in the chair, suddenly aware of its unyielding wood.

The first was from Medellín, a city teeming with poets apparently, and from its multitude one poet had become Daniel's friend. In his letter the man described a small scientific press he'd launched with a few university professors and also two new poems, and how inspiration came to him most mornings between 7.23 and 10.56.

Towards the end of the letter, the Colombian mentioned his brother, who'd recently moved to London with a woman from Uttar Pradesh. They had just opened a restaurant serving southern Indian cuisine. Would Daniel be so kind, the poet asked, to drop by for dinner one evening? If he mentioned his name he would surely get a discount. The instructions were vague — location: the second floor of a building above a porn shop in an alleyway in Soho — but, confident we would find it and always ready for a local adventure, we made a plan to go the following week.

Daniel reached for the next letter. My thoughts began to travel.

★   ★   ★

To me, poetry would remain hazy territory, and poets individuals who saw life through either microscopes or telescopes, people for whom there were a thousand ailments, a thousand medicine cabinets. They said they liked to climb but in truth they preferred the

64

descent. When I met Daniel he had one entire collection, endlessly polished and ready for the world, yet little desire to publish. Citing his favourite Czech author, he pointed out that neither Christ nor Socrates had ever written a line yet their teachings were still alive, while there were many writers who were read less and less in inverse proportion to the number of books they published. History, not critics and booksellers, would decide.

At the insistence of a friend Daniel had sent his first collection, *Lamentations in Front of a Closed Shop Window*, to a press in Manchester. A young editor had liked it, her colleague, also a young editor, had liked it, but it came to a sobering halt in the hands of the senior editor, who complained about what he called an abundance of Latinate words. There were several back-and-forths. After the senior editor suggested Daniel turn to a more Anglo-Saxon vocabulary and get in touch when he had a new collection, Daniel swore that from then on he would write only for himself and his friends.

Apart from his notebooks he had, over the years, committed lines to napkins, pamphlets, museum maps, tickets for different transportation systems, flyers for clubs, restaurant menus, place mats, gum and mint wrappers, shop receipts, margins of newspapers, and whatever else contained a blank space, including the fronts and backs of his hands, the safest place of all apart from the time he forgot and washed his hands and lost a poem to the drain.

Perhaps owing to my ignorance, or to caution or discretion on his side, Daniel showed me mostly fragments. This was fine with me; I had trouble concentrating when something was read out loud so the shorter the piece, the less chance of drifting. On the back of a cinema ticket: *Mortal coughing in the antechamber*. On the pamphlet to the Imperial War Museum: *Life in limbo, a stalling of haikus*. On a napkin from a café in Soho: *Canary in cage/Biography in microscript*. On a torn piece of paper: *Verbs locked away/The snow leopard's winter hoard*. On another scrap: *Lame dragon December*, followed by two smudged lines.

Some poems had been inspired by things he'd overheard at the museum, words spoken by visitors walking past or standing at a painting nearby, and in some cases, or actually most, they were direct transcriptions of phrases misheard, for that's how a new idea would pop into his head, he said, when he was there at his post, half present half absent, and phrases were being uttered around him. He could interpret them as he chose, and in many cases he jumbled them up, changed a word, replaced a letter or subtracted a line. He'd only started this methodology at Tate Britain, snatching things from the air and giving them shape with his pen. At the National Gallery there were too many visitors and too much noise and activity, so fewer chances to eavesdrop. I would often hear snippets of conversation as people entered and exited the rooms, like the details from paintings they sold on postcards in the shop, but my hearings and mishearings rarely led to anything new.

★ ★ ★

Daniel never asked for my opinion and I never offered one. Years ago I'd nearly killed our friendship by suggesting I didn't like something and had kept quiet ever since. It made little difference how much I listened or let my thoughts stray. Along with the nautilus, I was simply another ear, and sometimes all he needed was to get the poem off the page and into the air in order to then send it out.

The afterlife of what he wrote depended, I knew, almost entirely on the reactions he received through the post. When a poet from Buenos Aires expressed in the most diplomatic terms possible his concern over

Daniel's new collection *The Singed Fur of the Circus Tiger*, suggesting it was maudlin at times, Daniel immediately shelved it. He omitted 'at times' from his memory and pulled the word 'maudlin' into relief. Yet if he'd asked me I would've said, Don't shelve it, send it out. If he'd asked me I would have told him that I loved the poem about the old elephant that escaped a travelling circus, one of the few he'd read me complete, how after a life in chains and goaded by rods, four-ton Dora was startled by a cat and broke free and ran out into the highway where she collided with a bus. The driver died, Dora died, as well as six passengers, their wounds described in chilly detail. Daniel ended the poem with a description of the final spotlights to shine on the lifeless pachyderm, those of passing cars. But the poet from Buenos Aires wasn't moved, not by Dora or any of the other unlucky animals featured in the collection, and maudlin was too weighty a verdict.

It was nearing eight by the time Daniel put away his various papers and remembered I was hungry. By then I was shifting in my seat every few minutes and looking out of the inky squares of the windows. The pot of tea and the bottle of wine had long sat empty. After consulting a few takeaway menus we ordered three Thai dishes, clutching at our chopsticks in the half-lit room, the open container of rice sitting on someone's Collected Works, as Daniel asked me about my week and I about his. That was how many evenings, after the long show and tell, drew to a close.

★　★　★

My Sunday, I couldn't help feeling, had ended up being a long immersion in other people's pursuits and desires. I wanted to steer my thoughts elsewhere, away from bats, poems and corsets, so on the bus home I reached back in time to a correspondence of my own, the only one of my life, in fact, begun in my late adolescence and lasting into my early twenties.

Hatched not from a hobby or a mutual friend but from a pen-pal scheme I'd read about, with inmates at prisons in the UK. I filled out a form and sent it in. Based on my answers, a match was made. David Murphy was his name, an inmate at Wormwood Scrubs, a Category B prison in West London. I wrote him my first letter. Three days later, I received a reply. I no longer recall the contents, only my crackling pulse as I extracted the paper from the envelope. I sent him a second letter. A further reply. Each letter of his was a bit longer, more detailed.

Soon we were writing every week.

Most of his letters described life in prison: the soul-crushing routines, glimpses of the sky through three glass panes and wire mesh, drab variations in the food, highly volatile cellmates. Days measured out in steps — five from bed to door, three from bed to window, two from window to sink. A constant twilight. Pet spiders and mice. The fitful buzz of a dying fly. Occasionally he'd half joke about his situation or draw pictures in the margins. In his previous life he had worked as a welder.

I sent photos of myself, the most flattering ones I could find, and imagined them taped to the wall by his bed or stowed under his mattress. He never told me why he was there. I never asked.

A few months into our correspondence, David Murphy changed address. He was being moved, or ghosted, to Belmarsh, a Category A prison in Greenwich for prisoners whose escape would pose a serious threat to national security. I found this out later. At the time, the name Belmarsh sounded like a stately home, much more elegant than Wormwood Scrubs, so I assumed it was a nicer place, for more refined criminals.

It was clear we would never meet. Every now and then I'd offer to visit but he never responded to my question. I finished school, started university, dropped out, moved to London and began at Compendium, then at my second job, then my third. I dated appropriate and inappropriate individuals, moved flat and flatmates. Through it all, I continued writing to David Murphy.

And then one summer's night I was skimming the news on the BBC website when I read that two convicts, both jailed on multiple charges of murder, had escaped from Belmarsh that evening. Across the country search parties (dogs, helicopters, sirens) had been dispatched. A telephone number was provided should anyone have leads. For the first time ever, I saw his face. As a mugshot on the computer screen. It was haggard, but not in the way I'd imagined. He had lots of stubble, and his hair wasn't as long as I'd pictured it, in fact he had a close prison shave. But his eyes were what startled me the most.

Panic set in. He knew exactly where I lived, the address of my current flat and all the ones before. Of course he would come looking for me, perhaps even ask for shelter. I packed a suitcase and went to stay with friends in Forest Hill. I checked the street, peered out of every window, was tempted to change name, job, city.

Yet David Murphy never came. In fact, I never heard from him again. A small part of me was, I admit, disappointed, and for a time I kept half hoping he would pop up somewhere, that I'd turn a corner and there he'd be. As far as I know he has yet to be caught. It's unlikely he stayed in the country. He probably jumped on a freighter and is now in the wilds of New Zealand or Brazil, where he's started a new, sanitised life, maybe even a family. Every now and then, I wonder.

5

After so many years at the job I considered myself an expert in the sounds produced by different shoes on wooden floorboards. Clogs were the loudest but had gone out of fashion. So had most platforms and cowboy boots. Sandals with cork-filled soles made the least noise. Trainers too, nearly inaudible. Boots with traction produced a muffled crunch, like dog paws on snow. Heavy boots with metal buckles, usually on the feet of long-maned men from Scandinavia, sought an audience as much as the paintings. There must've been a shift in footwear over the years however, since the old-fashioned click clack so familiar in films had been generally replaced by less dramatic entrances.

Whenever I felt like detaching myself from what was around me, rather than listen for shoes I'd try to block out all sounds and focus on the reflections of visitors in the polished wooden floors. Every visitor at the Gallery has a double that wanders through the rooms with him, and in rooms where the wood is especially shiny the reflected double is nearly always more vivid and beautiful than the human above. As the afternoons wore on and the reflections diminished, my attention would then move to the shifts in light, and I would try to guess how long till closing time without checking my watch.

Shadows and reflections would've been different in my great-grandfather's day, when Gallery illumination was an evolving theme. With the lanterns that were first used the pictures received too much light, he said, and visitors could see their reflections in the protective glass more than the pictures themselves. Skylights proved much better: light poured into the centre of the room, bringing the work to life.

In Ted's day, too, there was no rotation, nor female warders. Heating came into existence rather slowly; certain draughty rooms lay in the dreaded pneumonia wing. Overcrowded London elbowed its way into the rooms of the Gallery. Warders had to rise from their chairs when spoken to, figures on standby that would go from L to 1 when addressed and from 1 to L when released, a constant movement between upper case and lower. Fog or darkness could cause the Gallery to close at short notice. Outside, horses would stand hitched to carriages for hours like thaumatropes at rest. All these details never ceased to have a hold on Ted and as they had a hold on Ted they had a hold on me.

Even in his twilight, when I would visit him in his two-room cottage in Yorkshire, my great-grandfather would return to the events of 10 March 1914. He had heard some of the commotion the suffragettes had been making, of their ardent campaign for the female vote, but had never imagined he would witness anything so dramatic first-hand. Mary Richardson provided Ted with the story of his life. Even the events of the Great War did not diminish the moment this young suffragette, drum major for the Women's Social and Political Union's Fife and Drum Marching Band, took a chopper to 'his' Venus; this story belonged to him, though it failed to make him a hero.

As a young girl I would listen on, fascinated yet pretending to be horrified, as he explained how the suffragettes were to blame for the collapse of society as he knew it, and how these national outrages, as he called them, were harbingers of the great European disorder to come. Even if he *had* caught her in time that day, it was too late. There was already disorder in the nation. Disorder in the Gallery. Disorder on the Continent. It was all linked, Ted would say, all linked. At the heart of everything lay grief and disorder, and swishing through this disorder was a phalanx of long, intransigent skirts.

His tone was so grave and prophetic, I rarely questioned anything he said, forgetting the cramp in my leg as he spoke about how in those years he was the first to admit that life as he knew it, meaning *his* England, would never be the same. It began with those viragos, he'd tell me, comets detached from the firmament, deviant and sharply veering, long-haired vagabond stars, hissing through the universe on their solitary paths, a tear in the social fabric, threats to the status quo. Yet once war broke out, Ted said, their battle, eclipsed by larger events, became no more than one of many lit matches in the stratosphere.

By then he had entered so far into the past, a brittle figure collapsed into his armchair travelling through decades when he scarcely had the strength to cross the room, that all I could do was let myself be pulled along with him, even when I'd heard the stories countless times and wasn't sure what to make of them, feeling more excitement than dismay. My affections had skipped two generations; I was never close to anyone in my family and he was the only relative whose stories ever really enthralled me.

In his head he was always turning them over, a mental exercise during which he rarely stumbled on a fact or figure. Winters when I'd visit we would sit by the radiator, and every hour or so he would place a coin in the palm of my hand to feed into his meter, as if the retrieval of his memories depended on it. He would tell me of the night in early May 1910 when Prime Minister Asquith, aboard his yacht the *Enchantress*, received news that King Edward VII had passed away. Saddened by these tidings, Asquith went out on deck and gazed into the darkened sky. At that moment, Halley's Comet came blazing overhead like a lit sword. There was our prime minister, alone with this punctual omen in the night sky, while in those years, back home, other fires were being kindled.

Comets and suffragettes. Ted always equated the two. He feared the approach of these comets that drew nearer, their brightness increasing, the light of their nucleus ever more vivid, great curvatures of tails stretching across the heavens, a sudden advance in size and splendour. One glimpse, one omen, that's all it took: decades later, the events of those years still had him in their grip.

★   ★   ★

Ted had been pacing in my thoughts that afternoon when the art restorer entered the room with her students. Along with my great-grandfather, it would be this woman who, in Room 65 of the Sainsbury Wing, shed light on an obscure aspect of the museum.

Mid-fifties, attractive, with straight chestnut hair, she stopped in front of a small van Eyck, an intriguing portrait of a man in a red turban, possibly the artist himself, a painting I had always liked despite knowing little about it. The students fanned out like apprentice surgeons at a dissection and pinned their eyes on the subject.

From my chair, I watched and listened.

'Paintings too are vulnerable to the ravages of time,' the restorer began. 'They crack and they flake, their colours change, things fade or darken. Any work you see today will have looked rather different when it was created. And if you look closely — not too closely — you will note that just about every painting in this Gallery contains a vast network of cracks.

'And these cracks,' she went on, 'are what we call craquelure.'

She spelled out the word. A dozen hands took note.

'Inherent craquelure, the release of stress, occurs with age. As you know, most of the tension in a painting is located in its four corners. Accidental craquelure, such as spiral cracks and spider cracks, is the result of external impact.'

The hands continued to scribble.

'Look at this van Eyck. Your attention is probably first drawn to the red turban, to the magisterial way in which each fold has been painted. From there, you move onto the face. It is more cracked than wrinkled, you can see — the paint's age shows even more than the man's.

'This type of grid craquelure is created when primary cracks, which follow the direction of the brushstroke, and secondary cracks run in right angles to one another. Aging cracks often follow the lines established by drying cracks. Remember: *mechanical forces will always seek out the path of least resistance.*'

Some students leaned forwards, pressing dangerously close to the van Eyck. My impulse to intervene and ask them to take a few steps back was crushed by my fever to hear more.

'Over time,' the art restorer continued, 'I hope you will all learn to identify fake craquelure, which forgers add to a painting in order to give it the illusion of age. They scrape the edge of the canvas on a table, bake it in the oven, and sprinkle sugar on top until the surface cracks in just the right way. There are other techniques too, but this is one of the simplest and most effective.

'Yet in the words of the great Friedländer, *Forged craquelure is arbitrary, monotonous and pedantic — whereas natural craquelure throbs with rich variety.* So, to conclude: craquelure grants a painting its history, its authenticity, a whole topography the painter himself could never have envisioned . . . '

When they left the room twenty minutes later I closed my eyes in order to process her words. Like a hot grille, the image of the van Eyck pressed into my eyelids despite the cracks being indistinguishable from where I sat in my chair. After hundreds and hundreds of hours in the Gallery, how had I failed to consider something so vital? I had always been drawn to decomposition, to the knowledge that everything in the universe tends from order to disorder, and the thought of the arrow of time also moving through paintings overwhelmed me. Painters create order from disorder, but the moment that order has been created, the slow march towards disorder begins again.

I'd been handed a secret. Visitors could stand and admire what they saw on the walls, point out to one another the various colours and compositions, but my inner lens would now be focused on something more hidden,

80

an intimacy between me and the paintings that a thousand gazes could not disturb. I had always sought quiet in the world and there were few movements quieter, I realised, than paint cracking over time.

* * *

Days after the art restorer's visit those three syllables — cra-que-lure — continued to rumble in my head. The allure of the crack, the lure of the crackle, the lair of the kraken. The crack of dawn, the crack of doom.

* * *

Little by little, I began to notice small changes in mood. At home, I felt ever more susceptible to things around me, above all to the abundance of creams, oils, facial masques and body lotions that Jane kept in our bathroom, combatants against the passage of time. Ever since I'd known her she'd been spending a small fortune on this mission to keep her skin supple and smooth, tender and silky for *the one*, and now each time I entered I felt the jars and bottles mocking me with their sweet pungent scents. In the past she'd been drawn to unavailable characters — men paralysed by depression,

81

addicts or alcoholics, urban hermits or living overseas; there was always something safely in the way, an expiry date stamped on the package. And once one man was out of the picture, it took a while to erase the rough Braille he'd left on her looks and perfect herself for the next. But now, perhaps, if she *had* met *the one* she could relax the campaign.

Meanwhile, in our flat, the moths continued to gather thickly. Jane laid out more traps, now in all the rooms, strips on the tops of cabinets, dressers and wardrobes. Yet the ones on my landscapes weren't decomposing rapidly enough, stubbornly resisting disintegration as if aware they would be replaced the moment they showed so much as a tear. Morning and night I would check for developments but no, these little brown torsos and wings remained intact, holding fast, in one final stance, to their makeshift landscapes.

★ ★ ★

At work I found myself challenged by ever greater feats of self-control. My patience was tested in new ways. For instance, I was both startled and not a little annoyed to note the presence of a new painting in Room 86 and the absence of one that'd hung there for as long as I had been working at the National Gallery. It was typical of curators not to let guards know about changes — overnight, paintings would be switched around or taken down and the next day you would send someone to the wrong room to see a painting that was no longer there.

In the Sainsbury Wing, one of the first things our new director had done was move the location of the *Battle of San Romano*; he decided the Italian paintings should be shown chronologically and that this Uccello should come earlier, so one day we arrived at work and saw it had been moved from Room 55 to 54. Ever since, people have walked past it. Had we been asked our opinion we would have told him that its original place on a wall that could be seen as one approached from several rooms away was more powerful than its current peripheral location. But no one takes our views into account.

During my tea break I went down to Human Resources and complained about the change in Room 86, struggling to contain myself as I explained that in order to do our job well we needed to be kept up to date on every alteration in the Gallery, that they ran the risk of making their guards look like fools by keeping us in the dark, and that if it were ever repeated I would resign, a lie naturally but I wanted to throw in some drama to make more of an impression. The woman nodded from behind her desk, glancing over at her colleagues to see their reaction, everyone was absorbed in a task, and she said *note taken* without taking much note, and before I knew it, it was time to get back to work.

★ ★ ★

Thursday was especially relentless. From room to room, post to post, a weary transference of grey as my colleagues and I released ourselves from one position and slipped into the next, rooms chairs thresholds, thresholds chairs rooms, as we carried out our silent musical-chairs rotation.

At half past four, time seemed to decelerate to an unbearable pace. Rotation didn't solve anything. In each room the minutes got caught in the same thick transparent gel. Searching for signs of movement, I studied the visitors. A hunched man in his seventies wearing trainers and a plastic rose ring — a retired actor perhaps, or a famous painter, or a tourist from Miami. A woman with cropped black hair and bright red glasses who kept checking her watch as if about to run off. A fat man with his shirt hanging out of his trousers, who seemed perpetually short of breath, stopping to pant in front of every painting. It was often tempting, and all too easy, to transfer a bad mood onto others — all I had to do was go up and scold someone for standing too close to a painting when they'd been keeping a respectful distance and then ignore their protests. I considered approaching the woman in red glasses just for some variety but she left before I had the chance.

A couple walked in and went to stand in front of paintings at opposite ends of the room. They moved anticlockwise, overlapping only once at a painting in the centre, and finished at the same time, then floated silently into the next room. Not long afterwards another couple, far less silent, the man pontificating without breaks, entered and exited the room, leaving behind a different kind of mood.

Two young Italians, one in a wheelchair, appeared, speaking loudly. One could tell they were brothers, they had the same forehead, the same curly dark hair, the same pitchy eyes, but the one in the wheelchair had a larger, more distinctive nose and was therefore more handsome. Each time his brother wheeled him before a painting he would crane his neck and try to make himself higher, a casualty, along with children and small people, of the established dictates of museum height. Yet his brother kept pointing at things from an angle that ignored the constraints by which his sibling was bound. Each time he pointed, the other one strained to see, and I fought the urge to walk over and gently intervene by perhaps suggesting one brother hold the other up to what he wanted to show him rather than futilely point it out, but instead I kept still, tapping my foot once or twice.

A large group entered next, a flock of tourists straggling behind one of our so-called educators in a tour organised by the Gallery. I stood up from my chair, straightened my tie and aimed at total verticality, feet parallel and back columned with wall, and waited to see whether my efforts would be acknowledged. But not once, as the guide began waxing on and on about the 'unequivocal musicality' of a certain painting, did he so much as glance in my direction. I knew he had seen me — after years of working at the same place, the wiles of others were familiar — and that afternoon he went as far as to comment on the female gallery assistants, so drab amidst the mythological women around them. A few visitors looked timidly in my direction but most were kind enough to ignore his attempt at humour.

Guy Mount had been tour guide for nearly as long as I'd worked there but we only occasionally, luckily, crossed paths. He drew a clear and unconcealed distinction within the staff and looked upon us security folk with disdain, his rust-coloured eyes peering down from his educated heights, oblivious to the sophisticated thoughts that might, just might, be flowing through even our minds every now and then. He was the sort of person who said nasty things with a smile.

Every institution has its visible side and its invisible one, and our Gallery was no different. We guards inhabited both realms, occupying backstage and front, though more the front, and the Gallery's image depended on us. Curators and directors meanwhile remained behind the scenes, dispatching important decisions from somewhere below. Guides were a third category in between. They felt superior to us yet inferior to the curators, and moved freely between above and below, deferential towards those who knew more, terse with those they assumed knew less. Most of them were cordial. Except for Guy Mount.

And each time we overlapped in a room, my ears were forced to listen as he raised and lowered his voice, especially loud when he sensed the visitors' excitement, then down once he had their attention, then up again the moment he caught sight of someone drifting, then down once he had them back. That day his voice seemed to issue from somewhere beyond, as if he were speaking through many characters at once, a deck of worn, greasy cards in which the top one acted as mouthpiece for those stacked beneath.

I sensed a current travelling up my right arm, electricity waiting to short-circuit and run amok, and I struggled to contain my anger, forcing a smile when two completely disoriented teens came up to ask after the room with the Hogarths. Something like heartburn flared up at the centre of my chest. An animal was awakening, cracking its joints and flexing its claws. Yet by some magical force, or perhaps simply through channelling Ted, for he would've resisted confrontation and accepted his position within the hierarchy, I managed to contain myself.

★　★　★

What they failed to ask at my job interview nine years ago was whether I ever entertained violent thoughts, to which I would reply, today, *Yes, all the time, and more so with every passing hour*. How not to occasionally envision the Gallery as a great locus of violent acts, a potential arena of destruction at both the paint layer and the human?

When I went to stand in front of Venus my eyes could only focus on the network of cracks, a shawl of time draped over her shoulders and running down her back, the paint thinned under so many gazes, especially male, the heaviest gaze of all.

As if to prove my point, a middle-aged man entered the room and came to stand in front of her, his oily pink face full of rapture. I withdrew to my post, a vanishing act in my grey uniform. After a few minutes of gaping he extricated himself from the spell and moved on, falling captive, before long, to another two-dimensional figure; even the most beautiful things, I loved to remind myself, carry out a limited conquest of space.

★ ★ ★

During my final shift I experienced yet more pulses of anger, the kind I have for the first day or two each time I quit smoking, when two girls entered the room laughing. One of them was punching things into her phone as she walked. If there was one thing I hated it was gadgetry, especially in the museum, and though the tiny plastic keys hardly made noise they always seemed loud to me. I bit my bottom lip as the girl stopped in front of me, ignoring my presence to the point that her right foot was nearly stepping on mine, and pressed a few keys. I was taller so could look straight down at the phone in her hand and see what she was typing. As far as I could tell, she'd composed one message, sent it off, and was now starting another. She ran through her list of contacts, her little fingers impatiently kneading the pad, and started yet another text. Grab the object and toss it across the room, I thought to myself, watch the screen crack into lightning bolts.

★ ★ ★

And then, like some kind of biblical release, a wonderfully familiar tune at a quarter to six: the jangling of keys. Just as on every other afternoon at a quarter to six, my colleague Henry came ambling through the rooms, hinting to visitors that soon our tiny kingdom would close. He jangled them loudly as he walked, indulging in his favourite moment of the day, when the sun set on our museum and everyone, native and from overseas, was ushered towards the door. There were always one or two individuals who hung back until the last possible minute, to buy the final postcard or see that final painting, and Henry would remind them they could return tomorrow but the reply never varied: they had an early plane or train to catch, this was their very last evening in London, they couldn't leave until, until, until . . .

At closing time, key jangling aside, I often thought back on old Dietrich, a former colleague. Dietrich had worked at Berlin's Gemäldegalerie, home to one of the finest painting collections in Europe, people say, for fourteen years before coming to the Gallery. He was with us for only ten months and then left under mysterious circumstances. He missed his old job too much and suffered from a 'devastating nostalgia', he confessed, for the paintings in the other collection. Everything, in fact, was about *the other collection*. At the other collection, there were many more Dürers. At the other collection, there were also more Cranachs (twenty-two to our eleven). At the other collection, the frames were less conspicuous. At the other collection, there were fewer tourists. At the other collection, people didn't talk so loudly in front of the paintings. At the other collection, they had a nicer way of announcing that the museum was closing. This last reminiscence was, in fact, what wouldn't free him.

I can't remember when it started — it must have been the day someone in the canteen inquired into how visitors at the Gemäldegalerie were asked to leave at closing time. Upon hearing this question, Dietrich's face lit up and he wiped his mouth with a napkin before explaining to all at the table that each afternoon at exactly 5.45 the museum would play the opening bars of *Ode to Joy* followed by a recording that would say 'The Museum will be closing in fifteen minutes' in German, French, English and Spanish. Between each language the same tune from *Ode to Joy* would ring out. After a decade and a half of listening to this morsel of Beethoven — without ever, he admitted, buying the recording and hearing the rest — it was etched in his mind like his own name.

It wasn't long after this conversation in the canteen that Dietrich started to look greatly disturbed whenever closing time approached. His face would cloud over and he'd grow distant and not reply when spoken to. Something was wrong, there'd been a shift in the Teutonic plates, and one day he stopped coming to work. Later, we were told a cousin had come to take him back to Berlin. That was years ago, when I first started working at the Gallery, but I'd still think of him at closing time.

* * *

After the *pushout*, museum-guard parlance for kindly requesting all visitors to leave, would come a quick sweep of the rooms to make sure no one had escaped our notice. The paintings fell out of focus; we searched for movement instead. After the halls were cleared, we would congregate in the vestibule for a final tally, some of us spent and still, others twitchy and impatient. Once everyone had been counted we would descend by the main staircase to our changing rooms and branch off into male and female. In a low end-of-day buzz, my colleagues and I would start to unzip, undo and unbutton, removing our grey and returning to civilians like a deflated army on reserve, no uniforms ever allowed to be worn outside the museum, and together with our male colleagues finally rejoin the city.

After going through the motions that evening for the 3,000th time, I exited into Trafalgar Square, reminded of the weather and whatever else had been taking place outside. The square's lack of coherence bothered me whenever I stopped to give it thought and in a perverse desire to prolong my bad mood I did just that, reiterating my dislike at having to contemplate anyone's back, from that of Admiral Nelson to Charles I and his horse, not to mention the back of whatever unsightly thing had taken up residence on the plinth. Everything faced Westminster instead of the Gallery and that day just to add offence the two fountains in the square had been stilled, decapitated sea monsters on which pigeons and tourists came to roost in even greater flocks than usual.

★ ★ ★

Daniel and I had agreed to meet in Piccadilly Circus to go to the Indian restaurant his Colombian friend had recommended. I walked up Haymarket and arrived a few minutes early, struck for the first time by how the layers of the fountain there, also stilled, could easily depict a few circles of hell. Towards the top was a ring of miserable carbonised pigeons, heads tucked in breasts. Below the pigeons, a ring of tourists breathing in city fumes. Below the tourists, a ring of steps coated with the muck of countless shoes from countless countries. Over these three rings, in a failed gesture towards transcendence, towered the statue of

Eros with a snapped bow. I caught sight of Daniel about to cross the junction and rushed to meet him before he came to me.

After so many years in London, I still didn't have a grasp on Soho's geography. The streets slipped through my fingers the moment I'd walked them regathering behind me like water, and I always had the sense that its residents and prowlers had a secret knowledge of the city's chambers, held up a mirror to places no one else bothered to look.

That evening the streets became a blaring blinking tangle of neon. Each turn felt like, and indeed was, the wrong one. At first I simply followed Daniel and his limp, assuming he'd looked up directions, but all he could remember, he eventually confessed, as Wardour turned into Frith and Frith to Greek, Brewer and Lexington, was something about a porn shop in an alleyway.

After following several false leads, his instinct proving no better than mine, we came upon an alley with rows of shops with blackened windows. Large, crimson XXXs blinked above the doorways and huge light boxes with pictures of naked women with stars on their nipples cast an erotic glow on to the pavement. In one upstairs window I spotted a woman's face looking down although she sat so quietly, I wasn't sure whether it was a woman or a mannequin. Her lips, candy-apple red, seemed poised to indulge every wish, yet there was something, perhaps her vacant stare, that didn't seem real. It looked strangely familiar and I wondered whether I'd seen it before, behind another window.

Below in the alleyway, large bald men in suits, seedy doormen of fulfilment, hovered in shop entrances. They stopped talking when we appeared, probably eyeing us as potential customers, and lit fresh cigarettes as they stood guard over the red velvety curtains that they alone had the authority to sweep aside, a parting of the curtains, a parting of the legs.

I glanced up at the window but the woman with the deadened gaze was no longer there. As we stood searching for the Indian restaurant amidst the flickering erotica, two peculiar men turned the corner and came ghosting down the alleyway like bodysnatchers on a mission. One was much taller than the other, he could have used his companion as a cane, and they both wore caps angled over their eyes. They passed uncomfortably close to us, I could hear the scraping of their leather jackets and smell the cigarettes they'd just stamped out, but their faces remained hidden and all I saw were their mouths, a dash and a smirk.

The men looked around before jumping into the XXX shop next door, the shorter one removing his cap as if in deference to Eros, a tastier version than the statue in Piccadilly. Once they entered, the velvety curtain fell back into place like a toreador's cape, obliterating all traces of their arrival. From the doorway of the shop opposite, the competition watched with envy.

Halfway down the row of peek-a-boo shops, whose aggressive lights diverted attention from their shoddiness, we discovered one building without any Xs. Its entrance, a corroded metal door with torn notices for live sex shows, stood ajar. We decided to go in. There was an unlit stairwell, the lights from outside falling on the first stairs but no further. I followed Daniel, who took tentative steps, raising his stronger foot first, then hauling up the other. As the building's concrete intestine wound its way past one floor and into the next, each lit by a frugal bulb per landing, we passed a pair of clogs laid out on a stair, as if someone had had second thoughts, removed his shoes and headed back down barefoot. The third floor contained only silence and two closed doors, so we forged onwards yet at the fourth and final floor there was no indication of a restaurant. I don't think either of us truly expected to find anything there.

On the way down I nearly tripped on the pair of clogs and when we reached the ground floor and stepped back into the night, the neon cries of the sex shops and the smoking vultures in the doorways seemed somehow unreal.

Yet right before leaving, I remember looking up at the upstairs window one last time and there she was, the pretty lady with the glassy stare, and I realised then why she looked so familiar. She reminded me of one of the mannequins in the Ed Kienholz exhibition they'd had a few years ago at the National Gallery. An intervention of sorts, they'd said, twentieth-century art placed alongside the old, and I'd been so intrigued by this installation, which took days to set up, unfamiliar flurries blowing through the halls of our museum, that once I heard it was complete I dropped by the Sunley Room on my first lunch break and wandered through the imitation crepuscule of Amsterdam's red light district, the trapped silicone whores gazing at me through the rain-streaked windows of their showcases, and I remember that as I hurried out, disturbed by the seedy crimson installation winking in our midst, I'd noticed a woman sitting quietly on a bench a few metres from the exhibition and wondered for a second whether she was part of the show before seeing it was one of my colleagues, suited and waistless like me, at her post.

★ ★ ★

We never found the Indian restaurant and, with my appetite ruined and Daniel's whetted, we ended up at Spuntino's, an Italian place in Rupert Street with loud music and young waiters with tattooed sleeves rushing about, two pounds for a Jack Daniels in a tin cup, five fifty for a small pizza. I think we were both relieved to be in a place where we could hardly talk against the punk volume of the music and the chaos around us, and not until after we'd eaten and stepped back into the night of Soho, flyers and rubbish blowing through the streets and the pageantry from pubs spilling out onto the pavement in a jumble of smoke and chatter, did I become aware of my desire to smash the panes of glass in the alleyway. Losing one's way is never unintentional, they say, there's a reason you take one street and not the other, pursue false leads or listen to bad directions.

★ ★ ★

Once home that evening I returned to my site. My latest landscape, still in its early stages, was a tiny model of an excavation, an idea I had after coming across a journal in our basement library describing various archaeological assessments of the terrain below the Gallery. The aim was to see whether there was a layer of dark earth capping the Middle Saxon material they'd discovered earlier and, if so, whether the distribution of artefacts within this layer indicated the presence of what they called ghost features. I was never able to find out what they meant by this, but assumed it was like the ghostly traces beneath a painting's top layer, early attempts the painter discarded, no longer visible but somehow still there.

My archaeological landscape proved to be more of a challenge than its predecessors. An eggshell wouldn't work — too domed and confined — and after casting my eye around for the right base I eventually found a rectangular plank in a skip outside a shop in Essex Road and sawed out a small rectangle on which I began to add the layers. For the Saxon gravel and sandy clays from quarry pits I used real sand, though it smelled vaguely of urine, from a playground nearby. For the dark earth sealing the Middle Saxon occupation I went to Cass Art and found brown paint the colour of burnt almond. For the shards of Middle Saxon glass I smashed up an ashtray with a hammer and created very fine bits, then selected the smallest sharpest fragments. Left only to recreate were the ribs of a cow, much of the skeleton truncated during the subsequent installation of a sewer somewhere in that terrain below the Gallery.

6

Over the past week a new idea had started to invade my mind, first stalking the edges and then gradually snaking its way to the centre and, as I thought about some of the more intense suffragette moments Ted had spoken of, this idea, bizarre yet increasingly logical, began to take shape: that much of history, or at least the history I'd been thinking about, had been carried out by the violence of the angle.

★   ★   ★

The angle at which Mary Richardson pulled on her tight-fitting skirt and parted her hair neatly to one side, the angle at which she fixed the meat cleaver up her left sleeve with the help of a few safety pins. The angle from which she approached the Velázquez, the angle of her wrist as she started to plunge her weapon into the painting.

Or, rewinding a few moments, the angle at which the workman's ladder was propped against the wall, and the angle at which the detective read his newspaper, and the angle at which light penetrated the skylight: each played a role.

And then with her extraordinary actions, Mary Richardson forced all these angles into a parallel, as she was intent on doing, a parallel between the public's indifference to the slow destruction of a prominent woman and the destruction of the financially valuable object of a painted one.

*　*　*

The angle at which metal tubes were jammed down suffragette throats and nostrils, their larynx and trachea, in the force-feeding campaign, the vertical assault of cold metal pressing against the walls of their oesophagi, despite the coughing and gagging a stream of food poured or pumped into their stomachs, mouths lacerated, teeth broken, digestive organs injured, bronchial complications to follow.

*　*　*

And the angle at which another suffragette, also armed with a meat cleaver, this one hidden in the folds of her purple cloak, rushed at John Singer Sargent's portrait of Henry James at the National Portrait Gallery, bequeathed by the author only months before. Mary Wood, who until the moment of the outburst had appeared a placid and unassuming old lady, shattered the protective glass and went for him in three separate places: below the right shoulder, on the left of his head, and on the right side of his mouth, fresh jagged lines wrecking the sitter's composure.

★ ★ ★

The angle at which an elegantly dressed suffragette outside Fortnum & Mason extracted a hammer from her fur muff and swung it at the glass of the window display.

★ ★ ★

The angles from which suffragettes were spied on in their cells through round peepholes covered with flaps, in every door of Holloway Prison.

The sweep of the pigeons at Holloway, cutting across in a loose angle, the hues of their plumage admired by Sylvia Pankhurst on her biweekly half-hour walks round the prison yard, their freewheeling command of the sky so at odds with the dulled gazes and plodding movements of the prisoners below.

A slight softening of hard angles in the presence of the matron, glimpses of humanity beneath her uniform as she stood in the distance, silent and watchful, with her chain and keys jangling at her side.

* * *

The angle at which a stream of ice-cold water was directed straight at Emily Davison, for fifteen minutes, when she barricaded herself in her cell at Strangeways.
The angle at which she flung herself over the railings of a balcony at Holloway, her attempt at suicide thwarted not by spatial miscalculation but by the wire netting thirty feet below.

* * *

The angles at which policemen pinched, wrung and twisted the breasts of suffragettes as they broke up the riot outside the House of Commons on Black Friday.

* * *

The angle of the collision between Emily Davison — who, until she stepped out onto the racecourse, had been standing beside

Mary Richardson at the Epsom Derby — and Anmer, the King's black thoroughbred, who came charging round the bend. The angle at which the hooves struck her chest, the angle at which blood gushed from the forty-year-old suffragette's nose and mouth. The horse somersaulted and landed on his jockey; both eventually recovered. Davison never regained consciousness and died four days later, on 8 June 1913.

★   ★   ★

And then, as if in response to her violent diagonal, the uncoiling of a tightly wound tension in a long horizontal, the unfurling of suffragette banners white purple and green. To the clamour of ten brass bands, the funeral procession wound its way from Victoria station to King's Cross, counting among its mourners Lilian Lenton, Harriet Kerr, Cicely Hamilton, Mary Leigh, Olive Bartels, Margaret West, Isabel Seymour, Mary Blathwayt, May Billinghurst, Vida Goldstein, Dorothy Pethick, Ada Flatman, Gladice Keevil, Clara Codd, Mabel Tuke, Dora Montefiore, Georgiana Brackenbury, Nelly Hall, Muriel Matters, Maud Joachim . . . That day my great-grandparents joined thousands of others to watch the cortège of

6,000 women, younger suffragettes in white carrying Madonna lilies, older suffragettes in purple and black carrying irises and peonies, and hunger strikers so frail they could only advance in small steps, an ethereal flock advancing to meet its fallen comrade halfway.

★   ★   ★

The unbending of an angle in a greater geometry of disruption. During those years all sorts of planes came together, dramatically intercepting, planes and elements that would normally never coincide. Canvas and cleaver, the shudder of steel instruments, the pounding heart of the racehorse, the trembling hand of a wardress forced to carry out the doctor's orders.

Decades after the Epsom Derby, after a life of many setbacks, the jockey Herbert Jones gassed himself in his kitchen; before his death he had claimed to remain 'haunted by that woman's face'.

★   ★   ★

What was I haunted by? At odd moments in the day or night I would ask myself this question, not too often but every now and then, especially when there were long lulls at work and no one entered the rooms I was watching over, or when I sat up late working on a landscape and larger, wilder moths drawn by the light of my desk lamp would rap at the window, or when I'd catch sight of my reflection in an unusual spot, such as in the glass panel of a painting or a silver plate in a shopfront or the tilted side mirror of a van.

Life's not complete without some kind of haunting. There on the very fringes of tranquillity, Daniel once said, should be at least one or two pacing wolves. I had chosen the suffragettes, they hadn't chosen me. Yet they were always somewhere in the margins. David Murphy, who for months after his escape threatened my dreams with a reappearance, had long been put to rest. The only ones with staying power were these women. But I couldn't help feeling that I'd inherited them from Ted.

★   ★   ★

One afternoon as I stood guard over Room 12, a room of Venetian painting, an essential room, its walls a deep scarlet, my thoughts began heading down the same path they always did when I was near a painting of St Jerome. What happened to the lion once the saint had died, I wondered, and what was the fate of animals generally after their owners passed away, my curiosity sparked one day in the museum bookshop by a reproduction depicting the burial of St Jerome. In the foreground monks prayed over the departed saint laid out on a slab while in the background hovered the diminished figure of the lion, a chopped off suffix, his great mouth open as if in a wail.

Like most St Jeromes, the Vincenzo Catena in Room 12 exuded a wondrous composure that I especially welcomed that afternoon. I hadn't slept well the night before and had a mild headache. Soft lines and soft colours, a flowing geometry, the saint deep in his reading, head resting on hand, his lion asleep on the floor while a quail pauses nearby. The painting had a stillness that few others in the Gallery contained, and was also one of the few where the image represented still drew me in more than its craquelure.

A woman entered from the far end of the room. With a few zigzags of the head she scanned the area, her reddish hair squirrelled into a loose bun that seemed to hold all kinds of information, and walked over to Titian's *Bacchus and Ariadne*, and from there on to the Catena. She stopped in front of St Jerome and, unless I was imagining things, her chest started to heave, the thick blue fabric of her shirt failing to hide the movement beneath. She raised a hand to her forehead, rested it there for a few seconds, then dropped it on her chest as she stared fixedly at, or rather, *into* the Catena.

I quickly took measure of the signs: breathlessness, increase in heartbeat, eyes possibly dilated. I sensed dizziness and vertigo, palpitations in the region of the heart, perhaps a ringing in the ears. The more I observed, the more convinced I was that this visitor was suffering from an ailment Daniel had once explained to me, specific to cultural sites where people felt lost, shipwrecked, overwhelmed. The museum controls the paintings, we try to control the humans, but no one can dictate the interactions between the two.

My first impulse was to lead her to a bench. My second was to remain where I was and see what happened. The woman sighed deeply, leaning her torso even closer towards the Catena as if wanting to disrupt the saint in his study. She was close, close enough for the painting to feel her breathing, but not close enough for me to intervene. Yet.

There were now four other visitors in the room but they seemed oblivious to the time bomb in front of them, who was now scratching her arm as if fumbling for something up her sleeve, and I debated whether to give orders to clear the room, clear the Gallery, clear the square . . . But the woman never gave me any reason to yell out those orders, or any order for that matter, and all I could do was stand and watch as she didn't attack the painting, didn't provoke me, didn't stir things up.

In a final taunt she leaned even further in, the upper half of her body hovering over the boundary delineated by the green cordon at shin height. I was surprised the alarm didn't sound, but before I could caution her she had leaned back upright, turned round and drifted off in a daze. At the far end of the room she gave the swinging doors a push and in doing so released a small draught, probably just enough to disturb the membrane of a painting hanging in the path of the current, its surface shifting ever so slightly. From my post I watched the door swing shut, once, twice, then vibrate a hairline more, before finally coming to a standstill.

7

An unwieldy tower of mugs filled with dirty water balanced against a small blue milk jug with a chipped lip upon four unwashed plates with sauce stuck to their faces beneath a jumble of forks and spoons and sharp little knives alongside two large pots, one with a burnt handle, the other with a burnt base, next to a strainer full of old tea leaves and a cereal bowl that'd grown a layer of whitish film. The kitchen sink grew busier by the day. Jane would eat in a hurry, at who knows what ungodly hour of the morning when she nipped home to bathe, feed and change clothes, and rush out again.

She and Lucian had begun seeing each other almost immediately. She hadn't been able to resist, and had returned to Camden Lock the following Sunday to buy her black scarf, inviting Lucian, along the way, to a Manorexia concert being held at Union Chapel on Upper Street that Wednesday, to which he said yes without any hesitation, she said, and during 'Armadillo Stance', the third song performed, she'd reached for his hand and from then on there was no going back.

Her tone was confessional, she halted at moments as if waiting to see my reaction, and more than once I had to reassure her that I didn't mind, Lucian had been someone I'd yearned for long ago, and I was only too happy, it was no exaggeration, to have been of help, however unintentionally. All the same, at first she only brought him over occasionally and spent most week-nights at his. I almost got used to having the flat to myself but refused to do her washing up.

★ ★ ★

The next Sunday at one of our locals, the Warlock and Essex, Jane entered a raffle and won a weekend away to a scenic town in the north of England. It had its own medieval wall, the pamphlet read, most of it still standing, and an impressive cathedral. Lucian wasn't fond of travel and had to remain in London for work. None of her close friends or colleagues were free. Jane turned to me.

As the train ribboned through the unframed landscape, Jane with her magazines and I bookless at the window, I wondered whether decades from now this scene would be replayed, two spinsters on our way to a small town somewhere to visit a provincial church and lay flowers on a grave.

According to the instructions, our B&B lay on the town's periphery, not far from the train station. Large disused warehouses huddled round us, their broken windows and blackened frames sullen reminders of their former lives. Despite the hour, a quarter past four in the afternoon, the streets were unusually empty and I couldn't help wondering whether the raffle committee was having a laugh, sending us two hours on a train to nowhere but an abandoned industrial town on the outer limits of existence.

But when we turned a corner and saw the imposing property with tall iron gates we thought we were charmed — not only to have won but in such grandeur — yet as we drew closer we realised our place was next door. Before moving on we set down our bags and peered through the bars, into a large landscaped garden with various pathways leading to a stately-looking home with an expansive façade. Above the entrance rose a clock tower with Roman numerals telling the wrong time. Trimmed hedges, bushes dotted with berries, tall evergreen trees. In the distance, a large man was advancing down one of the paths clutching a stick or a cane. Two women in oversized coats sat on a bench, knitting. In a rectangular airing court beyond them, two people were playing poorly coordinated badminton, not a single shot returned. Upon spotting us the man with the cane quickened his pace and headed in our direction. Worried we were about to be scolded for peering into private property, Jane and I picked up our bags and continued.

Modest in comparison to its neighbour, our B&B was an Edwardian semi, red brick with wooden shutters. We walked up the small path from the street and seconds after we rang the bell the door was opened by a woman with very short hair, a pigeon-neck silver. She introduced herself as Sam and led us into the foyer where another short-haired woman, this one with elfin eyes, introduced herself as Pam.

They congratulated us on our prize — each year their B&B was entered in the raffle — and asked us to sign the guest book. The last entry, a Mr and Mrs Honeywell, dated from two weeks ago. Sam insisted on carrying our bags and led us up a flight of stairs to a door with a carved number 3. Beyond this 3 lay a profusion of floral print. We paused in the doorway, still in our coats, and looked around. Curtains, bedspread, wallpaper: the blossoming decor seemed to advance in small leaps and spurts from one piece of furniture to another, the only pause the spaces between objects.

Sam deposited our bags on a fold-out table and informed us that breakfast would be served between eight and nine. We removed our coats and settled in. The room was a perfect little square, furnished with a queen-sized bed, two night tables, a fake leather armchair, and a balcony that over-looked a garden whose autumn trees, their crowns tossed in the wind, seemed to mock the inert vegetation inside. Above our bed hung a large pendulum clock with a pearly face and skeleton-like black hands. It was nearing five; I felt impatient for a walk.

After we'd made ourselves a quick cup of tea from a little tray, we set out. By then dusk had turned into an empty-handed magician who kept a few paces ahead of us, snuffing out the streets seconds before we reached them, robbing us of the sights we'd come to see. One by one, the lights in shop windows were switched off, café tables and chairs brought in, postcard racks folded up.

There was always tomorrow of course, our main time for sightseeing, but I'd been hoping for at least one memorable image to make the day feel complete. From nearly every street corner, grand and autonomous and immune to the setting of the sun, the spires of the cathedral, without question the town's centre of gravity, could be glimpsed. I looked forward to visiting, to wandering amidst the stone tombs of bishops, running our hands an inch above their carved faces, centuries of serenity transmitted to our fingertips, above us a heaven of stained glass windows, columns of rainbowed light.

It had been years since I'd visited a holy place — I once saw a man get down on his knees and pray at the Sienese crucifix in Room 51 — but the only time I ever felt in the presence of something holy, maybe even mystical, was when near Caspar David Friedrich's *Winter Landscape*.

That evening we dined at a pub, beer from a local brewery and overflowing jacket potatoes, and mapped out our Saturday. Cathedral — tea rooms — museum — tea rooms — city wall — pub. Jane had bought a map of the town though it seemed small enough to navigate on instinct. By the time we made our way back to the B&B the air had grown chillier, impatient nips of winter at the heels of November, and I remember walking close to her as we left the centre and returned to the outskirts, the warehouses with their gaping windows even more somber at that hour.

On our way out Sam had given us a key, just to be safe, she said, since they tended to go to bed early, at least by city-folk standards, and it had happened before that a guest was left standing outside for hours, frantically ringing the bell before either of them heard it since they both had remarkably deep sleep, she said, though Pam's had grown lighter lately due to a nervous disorder.

We softly let ourselves in and held on to the banister as we climbed the stairs to our room, moving through the strangely female silence of the house, a depth of silence that's only possible without men, the stairs lit by a small nightlight plugged into the wall between the ground floor and first.

Jane and I had never shared a bedroom but after four years of sharing a roof there was little awkwardness, and almost in tandem we slipped out of our clothes and into our nightwear, Jane to a short cotton gown and I into pyjamas. The radiators emitted a low hiss.

In the bathroom she lent me some make-up remover, a sparkly bluish solution, and afterwards I washed my face with the complimentary bar of soap. As I dried off, Jane, who'd been standing behind me waiting for her turn at the sink, asked whether Lucian used to bring women home when I was living with him.

I answered in the affirmative.

'Often?'

I paused, wondering whether to measure my response.

She reached for her toothbrush and applied a thick coat of paste, enough for three brushes, then turned to me.

'Well?'

'He went through phases.'

'How many women?'

'I don't remember.'

'Try to.'

I stared at our reflections in the mirror, each of us dark-haired and dark-eyed yet so different, my jagged fringe in need of trimming, her undulating mane that fell past her shoulders, my complexion whiter, hers on the yellow side, and thought about how many times we had gazed into the same bathroom mirror at home yet minutes or hours apart. Until then no mirror, I realised, had held both our reflections at once.

'Like how many, Marie?' she asked again and turned to look at me sharply, holding her toothbrush.

I'd give her the truth. 'I don't know . . . a hundred?'

'A hundred?! In two years? That's one a week!'

'Jane, he's a good-looking man. And he was young at the time, and single.'

She turned on the tap and ran her

toothbrush under it, brushed for a second, then removed it from her mouth.

'Handsome, single, whatever, he's a bloody liar. He said he'd only been with Carole, his ex, and then with Sue, another ex, and then with some girl from the Lock and then me. Maybe he's been lying the whole time, maybe he's up north with some girl this weekend, maybe he's just as jaded as all the others, who knows . . . '

No, I reassured her despite having no idea, No, I'm sure he hasn't been lying, I said, at most he's knocking off a few digits to appear more gallant, you really needn't worry, but Jane wasn't listening and again called Lucian a liar, this time a liar and a bastard, and as she spoke the water gushed out of the tap.

Each second, I began to feel, was killing a wave.

'It obviously wasn't only Carole, his ex, and Sue, his other ex, and who knows who else from the Lock, but a long string of them, I'm sure, and now he's probably somewhere up north with — '

'No, no, this was all years ago,' I said, and motioned to her to turn off the tap but she was too caught up in phrasing and rephrasing, repeating the same thing over and over by simply varying the sentence structure, to notice. I leaned over and shut off the gushing water.

'I haven't finished,' she snapped, and turned it back on.

★ ★ ★

The bed was large enough, or perhaps we were each small enough, to lie comfortably distanced from one another, my half separated by several inches from hers, a good thing since her nerves seemed more livewire than ever. Once I switched off the light she quieted down, mumbling one last thing about Lucian before falling asleep, and as I drifted off I imagined I was there on the sunken futon behind the screen in the old Camden flat, with Lucian somewhere beyond, on the sofa rolling a cigarette or reading one of his rock biographies, listening to Bowie at low volume.

★ ★ ★

Sometime in the early hours, most likely between five and six though I was never sure, I was awakened by a tapping sound. This tap was followed by another. And another. The taps came from the direction of the balcony.

'Marie, did you hear that?' Jane was already awake.

'Yes.'

Tap, tap, tap.

The taps were spaced out. Nature was not so methodical; it was not a branch being driven against our window by the wind.

'Do you want to go and see what it is?' she asked.

Tap, tap, tap.

Jane drew the blanket around her, pulling most of it off me, and said, 'Will you go and see? Please?'

In a sleepy haze, which curbed the adrenalin that would've otherwise been coursing through me, I crept out of bed, negotiating the sifting darkness of the room, and with cautious steps edged towards the balcony. I gripped the curtain and pulled it aside. A faint light was shining down from somewhere above, enough to exhibit the man standing there. His face was round and fleshy, his hair floppy and blond. Full-moon eyes peered past me and into our room. In contrast to his face, his body was long and willowy, arms dangling at his sides, and the overhead light created the strange effect of illuminating only his head and trunk as if they were floating without any bottom half, like the detached torso of a statue.

For some reason I didn't feel fear, only tremendous curiosity, and I got up as close as I could to study the apparition on the other side of the glass, mesmerised by this presence at once startling and remote. As I stood face to face with our visitor, whose saucer eyes were now staring straight at me and no longer beyond and into the room, my hand reached for the door handle. I was so drawn to this almost fantastical ghost of a man, an inverted shadow, its negative plate, that I hardly heard Jane calling out.

'Don't you dare!'

Only then did I turn round to look at her, the diluted light entering the parted curtains just enough to provide me with a glimpse of her face and the sheets, and it was only her shriek, which followed the words *Don't you dare*, that pulled me back into the present and made me take control. I let the curtain fall and tore myself away from the balcony, relieved once I'd left its force field.

I turned on a lamp. All the floral print sprang back to life. Jane raised an arm and pointed mutely in no real direction. I told her to stay put and remain cool, a tall command, I knew, but what else was there to say, and rushed out to fetch the women. After years of working in security there I was, face to face with a bona fide trespasser, and I went ahead

123

and did what I had been endlessly trained to do: go and raise the alarm.

Halfway up the stairs I ran into the women charging down.

'What is it?!' they cried, one by one or in unison, I no longer remember, as I jumped out of their way and watched them rush into our room.

Within seconds the curtain was drawn aside and the spherical face revealed. Watching from the bed Jane lay contorted and agape, one bare leg emerging from under the covers.

'Oh, it's this one,' said Pam or Sam (that night, they were indistinguishable), and signalled to her partner to release the curtain. The fabric rectangle fell over the gaze, cutting it off with a swish. The women told us not to worry and hurried out.

A minute or two later, the doorbell, followed by an exchange of words and footsteps on the stairs. Without a knock or any warning, two solemn men entered our room and went over to the balcony. One of them turned the lock and with a solemn hand slid open the door. The man outside put up no resistance. It happened so quickly, I barely had a chance to register him as he was led past. All I remember was the pale, fleshy face and the blond hair, a few tones lighter indoors, and how the lunar eyes had been emptied and lost their glow, and the bumbling shape of his long-limbed body, now attached to a pair of hesitant legs, and the blue pyjamas with a pocket on the breast. In his face, as he was led across the room and out the door, I saw the disappointment of a spectre that briefly enters the land of the living and is then ordered to return to his tomb.

By the time I joined Jane in bed, morning, a more assertive intruder, was forcing its way through the curtains, and I remember burying my face in my pillow to block out the light, overly aware of the thickening birdsong outside.

Before breakfast Jane asked me to check the balcony for signs of the night before. I too was curious, and went over to see. But there was nothing to report, no indication that a scene had been played out hours before, no footprints, no fingerprints, no trace. Beyond rose several very tall trees, half of them growing on the side of the B&B and the other half on the stately grounds next door. Beneath the wall that separated them, I imagined, their roots were deeply inter- twined.

In the dining room sat Pam and Sam, each with a mug of tea and different sections of the paper. Their expressions conveyed nothing. Yet after asking whether we had any special requests and returning from the kitchen with two heaped breakfast dishes, their calm unravelled. They began to explain, interrupting one another rather anxiously, that the building next door was a private asylum, and every now and then a patient would escape. But this was only the third time in eight years.

In the mid-nineteenth century, they continued as we started on our scrambled eggs, grilled tomatoes and mushrooms, a wealthy gentleman without partner or children lived in the house next door. For some reason, perhaps out of a desire for company, he decided to turn it into an asylum. He brought in a whole staff of doctors and nurses and opened his doors to the troubled. He would interview prospective patients himself, and offer a discount when moved by someone who was unable to afford the fees.

A great recreation hall was built, seventy feet long and thirty feet wide, Sam told us, where the doctors put on dances and theatricals. A bakehouse and joiner's shop soon followed. Days were filled with all sorts of activities, patients given small patches of land on which they could play Creator. Even those with severe concentration problems usually managed to raise something from the soil.

'In fact, they even had their own monogrammed china,' Pam said, gesturing towards our plates.

With a fork I pushed aside my remaining food until a dark blue seal came into view: CLOCK AND WATCHMAKERS' ASYLUM.

Jane shoved away her plate and leaned back in her chair. In order to compensate for her rudeness I kept eating though I wasn't used to large breakfasts and felt increasingly full. Just as Pam was starting to tell us about the dejected Welshman who had planted a hazel tree that still flourished to this day despite creating a digression in the garden, Jane turned to me and said, as if the women weren't there, 'Marie, I'd like to return to London.'

'Now?'

'Yeah, I don't want to stay in this town for another hour.'

'But we haven't seen anything.'

She shrugged. 'You can stay if you want but I'm leaving. I don't like the vibe.'

'What vibe?'

'I'm not going to stay another night, here or anywhere. *You* can.'

'Well no, not if you don't . . . '

Pam rose from her seat and began to clear the table. Sam remained seated, staring uncomfortably downwards.

'You can stay,' Jane repeated. 'But I'm leaving.'

'No, no, I'll come with you . . . '

We excused ourselves from the table, or rather, I excused us both, and climbed up to our room. Faded in the daylight, the floral print looked less zealous and oppressive. It was a shame to be leaving.

'Are you sure?' I ventured one last time.

'You can stay but I'm out of here. These women seem nice enough but I know when to read the signs. It's like when the pilot says, 'The weather at departure is stormy and the weather at our destination is stormy and we wish you a very safe flight.''

For some reason I started laughing, which seemed to push Jane further towards the edge, and I had to bite my lip as I folded my clothes into a bag. Before zipping up her toiletries case, Jane grabbed the remaining tea bags from the tray and threw them in.

Despite the awkward turn of events, the women shook our hands warmly and told us to please return, mentioning that their home looked especially nice in summer. Jane mumbled something incoherent, I said thank you a couple of times, and everyone breathed a sigh of relief, no doubt, once the door closed behind us.

As we wound our way back to the train station, circling the town centre one final time, I caught sight of the spires of the cathedral in the distance, now a hulking, majestic reproach.

★   ★   ★

The train hurtled past a cluster of industrial buildings only a shade darker than the sky. I thought of the patient returned to his asylum, and imagined the sound of different bells jangling in and out of tune, and of clocks attempting to realign their ticks and their tocks, preferring to imagine only non-human sounds, exercises in futility like trying to light a cigarette without cupping it from the wind. I wished we hadn't sent him back. Next to me Jane thumbed through a magazine, occasionally humming a tune to herself, one I didn't recognise, and only once did she look up, to show me a picture of a woollen black cape, saying they were coming back into fashion that winter. When we reached Euston station she asked whether I'd mind bringing her bag home and promptly jumped on a bus to Camden to go check on Lucian.

A moth flew past my face almost as soon as

I entered the flat, safe, so far, from the deadly strips lying in wait. I clutched half-heartedly at the air, aware it'd already flown off, and headed to my room, where my landscapes were waiting in the dark.

8

The sky that Sunday was marine blue in its upper regions, crossed by boatmen in white, and an empty waveless grey further down, as if the sun were uncertain what to give the last of November. As I walked the side streets of Pimlico I was struck by the emptiness of my path. I knew that part of town on weekdays and now saw that much of its life would withdraw come the weekend. Yet the place wasn't entirely empty, I soon discovered, for there ahead of me was a tramp kneeling on his blanket, a large red-and-green checked affair that occupied most of the pavement. I felt I was crossing someone's living room and intruding on a moment of privacy; he sat very still, a soiled paperback in one hand while the other gripped the neck of a large bottle of Lucozade. He didn't look up when I walked past, his head more or less at the height of my thigh, and I made sure not to step on the frayed edges of his blanket though from what I could see they were used to being trodden on. At his side a handsome bull terrier, some kind of Staffordshire and American pit mix, was sprawled out at half-mast alert, drowsy but attentive. In the tenuous light the broad curvature of its head looked especially soft and I longed to stop and run my hand over its fur but my instincts told me to keep walking.

Once by the river I slowed my pace and breathed in the heady mix of Thames air and car exhaust, the traffic moving more in time with the water than on weekdays. There was no hurry so I could wander; Daniel and I hadn't set an hour. He had begun working at his Tate most weekends, a decision that so far had benefited both his finances and his writing, he said, since the relatively empty rooms allowed him space and time to think outside the confines of his home, and had he gone to a library he wouldn't be making the extra cash.

It'd been years since I'd visited Tate Britain and as I walked beneath the row of bare chestnut trees that ran parallel to the river, every now and then stopping to take in the view of the few barges napping on the muddy Thames, I tried to remember which Pre-Raphaelites were in the collection, probably most of its finest specimens, but after a few minutes of envisioning pale knights and expressionless beauties, in my mind all with the same porcelain face, draped in medieval colours, I started to think about how strange it would be to see Daniel in their midst, and how his own irregular geometry might jar with the paintings around him, and from his lameness my thoughts shot back to the major story of his life, one he rarely mentioned, not his marriage, not his poems, not his catalogue of poet friends in other countries, but the one he told me shortly after we met.

⋆ ⋆ ⋆

It had begun with a headache, he said, one of those headaches that stamps out nearly every impulse and emotion, the pulse of an imp inside your brain. The headache arrived with the morning post, half a dozen envelopes scattered on the floor, nothing of interest a tiny voice told him, yet he bent down to gather them all the same. Just as he reached for the final item, an electricity bill, he felt a bolt of pain behind his right eye. He stood up, straightened his back and dropped his shoulders, but the pain was still there.

He placed the envelopes on his desk and got back into bed. He would wait for the headache to pass. After an hour, he called in sick to work and took two aspirins; a few hours later, he took two more and began to sense that something heavy and impenetrable had sprung up around his head, a complex fortification that pressed into his temples. He tried sitting up, lying down, one pillow, four, reclining at a ninety-degree angle, or at 130. As the afternoon stiffened around him, Daniel said, he imagined an immense ship sailing towards him, a ship carrying all the headaches he'd ever had in his life, closer and closer until its keel grazed the top of his head.

Day two was no different. He went to see his GP, who said it would pass. Yet on day three, the ship felt heavier. By day four, Daniel was desperate. The only thing that helped, just a little, was to chew strong peppermint gum on the side where it most hurt, behind his right eye. Along with this and extravagant amounts of aspirin and ibuprofen, he had tried every remedy he could think of: tiger balm and eucalyptus oil, hot washcloths and bags of ice, pressure showers and deep-tissue massage, a Chinese acupuncturist, a German reiki man. He wore sunglasses, avoided screens, monitors and the printed word. He wrapped a kerchief tightly around his head, otherwise it might split open. He tried whatever remedy people happened to put forward, from his local newsagent to the woman at Boots. Everyone had an idea. None of them worked.

At home, he felt outside time. Despite the painful fortress that imprisoned him, he refused to stay immobile. His search for a cure, a wise word from somewhere, wasn't going to happen while he lay in bed, so at least once a day he put on his sunglasses and went hunting for a solution.

Soon his extended family was discussing his condition. His cousin Lucy recommended a headache doctor she had once seen in Harley Street. Daniel went to this doctor and ended up parting with £135 for the man to tap his skull, shine lights in his eyes and wade through three pages of questions. He was sent home with a jar of ointment and a box of beta blockers. He rubbed the ointment into his temples, took the beta blockers. Nothing.

Day six, he ran into a friend on the street, Paul, who worked at the gift shop at the British Museum. It was he who told Daniel about the Hungarian hypnotist somewhere off Marylebone High Street who had cured his wife of chronic back pain. This man was an expert in pain, he'd said, knew how to make it vanish. On the spot, Paul called his wife and got the Hungarian's number. Daniel was on the next bus to Marylebone.

The Hungarian had thick white hair and blue eyes that seemed to hold half the sky. He wore rings, four fluted bands of silver, two on each hand, and wasn't particularly tall. Yet he carried himself proudly, Daniel said, as if he were taller.

'What is problem?' he asked.

Daniel removed his sunglasses and pointed to the right side of his head, describing the pain that wouldn't go away.

'No problem,' the hypnotist replied.

He then sat down and motioned to a stool across from him. Once Daniel was seated, he was instructed to look into the man's eyes, into his eyes and nowhere else. That was easy. As Daniel stared into the black pupils and their surrounding blue, he began to see a land of old forests and lakes, where clouds tiaraed round treetops creating ephemeral crowns, and houses wore hats of chimney plumes . . . For a second he thought he heard a woman yelling in a foreign language in another room, but blocked out the sound. And as he gazed into the distant landscape unravelling within that panoramic pair of eyes, the man asked him to count backwards from ten.

'Ten, nine, eight . . . '

From up close the hypnotist had a sweet, nostalgic smell, like black cherry tobacco. Daniel was tempted to lean forwards, he said, and inhale more deeply, but found he could not move.

'Seven, six, five . . . '

He was still aware of the Hungarian's breathing but could no longer see any landscapes in his eyes. His pupils had turned into two round black hats floating on the surface of the bluest water.

'Four, three, two . . . '

Once Daniel had finished pronouncing numbers ten to one, he had no idea where he was sitting, whether he was sitting at all, nor where he'd lain his hands, knew not whether they were at his sides or in his lap, and he couldn't feel his legs either, whether they were crossed or straight, whether he was still wearing shoes.

From somewhere deep and remote, like halfway through a mountain tunnel, he heard the voice of the hypnotist asking him to repeat, *Head does not control me.*

'Head does not control me . . . '

'Head does not control me.'

'Head does not control me . . . '

After this, said Daniel, he couldn't remember anything further. All he knew was that many minutes had passed and that he had travelled to a foreign land and returned.

A clapping of hands. The clanking of rings. Sounds from the street. The trance was over, his ache had vanished. His head could breathe again, the ship and the fortress had fallen away. After six leaden days, he had forgotten what it was like to be free of pain. And now, he was reminded.

'Thank you, my friend, thank you,' Daniel said, patting the Hungarian on the back.

The Hungarian raised a hand and said, 'No problem.'

'How much do I owe you?'

The man asked for £120, looking away as he said the amount, as if discomfited by monetary matters. Overflowing with gratitude, Daniel gave him an extra ten. The Hungarian beamed. They shook hands. Daniel put on his coat and started to walk towards the door. With the first step, and then the second, his left leg felt heavier and fell behind the right. He gave it a shake and continued, but again that leg fell behind. He tried putting the other foot first. But something wasn't synchronised. His feet refused to walk in the way they had for the past thirty-four years. He looked over at the hypnotist.

'No problem,' the man said.

Daniel limped out of the room and started down the stairs, clutching the handrail. Even the surface of each stair felt wrong, as if the world had redrawn its geometry. Out on the street, it was the same. He checked the pavement and saw it was even. It was his left leg that did not want to cooperate. It kept falling behind. Again, he tried placing that foot down first, then bringing the other forward. But the moment he stopped trying to coordinate them, the limp returned.

After a few days, he went back to Marylebone.

The hypnotist shrugged and said, 'Temporary. No problem.'

Over the next few weeks, Daniel sought out experts across London. They measured each foot and leg, tapped and weighed them, asked him to walk at different speeds, took X-rays and scans. Every doctor concluded the limp originated from his head. There was no asymmetry anywhere in his body, no trauma, tumour or inflammation.

Whatever the truth, the limp was there to stay. His headaches were gone but in the rewiring, Daniel said, something else had come undone. He had traded in the headache for the limp and, when it came down to it, life was more tolerable with the limp. After his visit to the Hungarian, and to this day, he has never suffered another headache. But every deficit of his, he told me, everything he hated in himself, would be spelled out in that gap between his feet.

He returned to the Hungarian many times. At first the man kept saying, *No problem*, and then one day he was gone. A week later an Austrian dentist hung a sign, changed the doormat, and set up shop in the space.

A chilly wind had started to whip along the river's edge. I lowered my face, drew my arms into my chest, and turned left towards my destination.

In my mind, museums and the law were tightly bound up and as I climbed the steps to the Tate I was reminded that it lay on the site of a failed Victorian prison, the radials of its panopticon design subjecting every prisoner to round-the-clock observation and a suppression of dialogue between inmates. Grim details, like the spyholes in each cell door fitted with eyelashes, never ceased to be an item of curiosity and horror. In 1890 Millbank Prison was torn down and before long a different sort of warder began to implement another kind of silence.

I stopped at the first paintings that greeted me but then decided that before anything else I should find my friend, who'd failed to tell me which section he'd been assigned. First I turned right, into Turner land, but he wasn't in any of those rooms so I crossed the hall and went left, wandering aimlessly past Blakes and Burne-Joneses, feeling nips at my conscience for not stopping to look, moving through the rooms like a train that slows down at small village railway stations, stalling just long enough for passengers to read the station's name and have an idea of what they might be missing before the train picks up speed and continues on its way. I had seen people do this constantly at the National Gallery, and always wondered what was so urgent that they couldn't slow down for even thirty seconds.

In a daze I crossed room after room, my steps quickening or easing up depending on the people and dimensions I encountered, for some rooms felt generous and immense and others like crowded annexes, until the image of Daniel, seated and uniformed in Room 9, a large hall containing works from 1850–1880, came into view. He didn't see me so I stopped to observe him, sitting with his legs crossed and head tilted back, as he kept an eye on a group of Russian tourists crowding round the wistful *Lady of Shalott*, a semicircle of gaping faces, only half of them focused. The guide waved her umbrella like a lion tamer and once she had her lions captive she lowered it and began to speak.

I approached from the side. Startled, Daniel quickly uncrossed his legs and said my name as if to remind himself who I was. The pen and notebook in his lap fell to the floor. He bent down to pick them up.

'Have you been getting some writing done?'

'A bit . . . It goes from silent to noisy back to silent.'

'I know. That's how it is.'

'I think the acoustics here are more pronounced than at the Gallery.'

I looked up and around. 'Could be.'

The Russians started to file out, led by their guide.

'Have they been here long?' I whispered.

'A couple of minutes . . . How was your trip?'

'I'll tell you about it later.'

'But how was it?'

'I'll tell you later.'

He shrugged. 'Okay.'

He'd sounded confused when I rang him that morning, and asked why I was already back in London. I'd said I'd explain when we met, that for now I just wanted to get out of the house and put my Sunday to some use, as I would have had I seen the cathedral.

'Come and see this one,' he'd said.

★ ★ ★

Familiar with the irksome sensation of sitting in a chair while someone towers over you, I said I'd have a look round and return before closing time. Daniel seemed to welcome the idea.

In the room hung a few works I recognised from childhood visits or textbooks, in every case the reproduction more familiar than the original: Millais' *Ophelia*; Hogarth's self-portrait with pug; Reynolds, Derby and Gainsborough . . . I greeted them silently, old acquaintances to whom I'd never given the proper time, so patient over the years, no reproach whatsoever, their existence as untouched by my life as mine by theirs. I liked the Turners most anyway, and those I hadn't even stopped to take in.

Just as I was about to move on to the next room and leave Daniel to his notebook, I noticed a painting I'd never seen before. Or perhaps it had simply never caught my attention in the past. But that day it jutted from the wall like some kind of promontory, forcing out a space for itself beyond the frame, and I went over for a closer look.

Pegwell Bay, Kent — A Recollection of October 5th 1858, read the caption, by William Dyce. It was a mysterious painting, of a seaside landscape with a few human figures, and my eyes first came to rest on the wall of ancient wrinkled cliffs resembling a procession of tired elephants. The shallow inlet was like a lunarscape, with rocks and

143

boulders emerging from a glinting yet motionless body of water. Clumps of seaweed, rocks covered in moss, an old fence run aground, a pole measuring the level of the tide: details I noticed a few moments later. The human figures in the foreground — three women and a boy (the painter's son, wife, and her two sisters collecting shells, the sign explained) — had an otherworldly aura. Most disconcerting of all was the boy, his spectral face as pale and distant as the cliffs.

Over the years I'd fantasised about stepping into many a landscape, of following paths that led far beyond view, but I would never wish to step into this one.

Upon seeing me at the painting, Daniel came over with his notebook under his arm and asked whether I had spotted the comet, to which I said no, startled by both the thought of a comet in a painting and the fact I had missed it. I leaned closer in to scour the sky — gradations of light pink and blue thinning into yellow, like a molten version of rock sediment, dolomite, limestone, sandstone and shale, and finally found the comet. A simple white brushstroke: one milky line at the top, hardly visible.

Daniel told me that Donati's comet would not pass over Earth again until the year 3811. In other words, this was one of the rare glimpses we would get, here in Dyce's painting. The last time it had passed over our planet was in the autumn of 1858. On 5 October, the date in the title, the comet was at its most brilliant — at twenty minutes after sunset, its head could be seen with the naked eye.

As I gazed at the astral body, its opal white streak growing ever more important and distinct in my mind like a fiery ice-cold sword rising up and away from the canvas, Daniel went on to describe how on that day crowds had thronged the streets, rooftops and bridges to catch a glimpse of Donati, which was not only the second brightest comet of the nineteenth century but the first comet ever to be photographed.

'No matter how greatly you shine,' I later said to Daniel in the pub, 'it's all over before you know it. And what's left? A white brushstroke, only visible if you really look.'

'That's better than nothing.'

'Well, most of us don't even leave behind a brushstroke.'

* * *

Yet that faint brushstroke skimming the surface of the canvas didn't exit my thoughts for a while and, looking back, I couldn't help feeling like events that winter were somehow harnessed to its tail, as if my glimpsing it that day were a tiny, punctual omen of its own. A comet in a painting, how sad to fall prey to such superstition, and when I went back months later and found in its place William Holman Hunt's *The Ship*, dark and metaphorical but no Pegwell Bay, I went to demand an explanation at the information desk, where someone eventually mumbled a few words about loans to other museums due to the bicentenary of Darwin's birth.

9

And then, one glorious afternoon, she returned. With fewer students, six in all, and a magnifying glass. The students too were equipped with magnifying glasses, I noticed, medium-sized discs with large black handles that they clutched as they stopped and waited for their mentor to speak.

Since her last visit I had thought many times about how a painting went from being a thing of beauty to a thing of decaying beauty to a thing of decay. Our museum must have held countless instances of paint giving in to tension, loosening its dominion over faces and landscapes, handing them over, instead, to the paintbrush of hours, and I still harboured the plan to one day go in search of as many examples as I could find.

The art restorer cleared her throat and tucked an imaginary strand of hair behind an ear. She reminded her students, who had now formed a small circle around her, of the anatomy of paintings — support, primer, paint layers — and how each of these parts had its own movement, islands of paint shifting all the while on something softer than the top coat. Information they seemed familiar with; they nodded, as if impatient for her to continue.

From there she went on to discuss the various types of craquelure, how one type of crack could be distinguished from the others, and the myriad ways in which it might have come into being. She repeated some of what I'd heard last time. She also spoke about drying cracks in the form of flames, nets, brushstrokes, spirals and grids, and ageing cracks in the form of spokes, garlands, corn ears and diagonals.

All tension spreads outwards once a unit has been disturbed.

Once she had run through her list, the students went in pursuit. This time all the paintings in the room were thrown under scrutiny, not just one, the cracks sought after like rare butterflies whose patterns could only be appreciated from a certain perspective.

At first I didn't know which way to turn. Each student was at a different painting. The restorer took her place at the centre of the room keeping a gentle eye on things, and every now and then would smile over as if to thank me for my patience. She needn't have, however, for I soon saw I had little to worry about. With rare restraint, the students maintained a good distance from the paintings and none held their magnifying glass too close to a surface.

As they stood happily, or perhaps anxiously, inspecting, I went through the list of cracks that had just been recited and started to envision them in the people around me.

Upon closer observation, the art restorer didn't seem as serene as I'd first thought. She kept clearing her throat and tucking strands of hair behind her ears when none had fallen out, and I saw at the centre of her chest a concentric spiral crack, similar in structure to that of a star group, one great swirl from which the primal energy of the universe might come radiating outwards.

In the male student to her left, his narrow blue eyes squinting in concentration, I saw horizontal brushstroke cracks running across his face as if following the grooves of the brush in the paint layer, like fine currents of wind marking his cheeks.

Next, I observed a young woman in a seahorse-print dress who kept polishing her magnifying glass on her sleeve, surely something she wasn't meant to do. On her neck, right above the collar, I located a large spoke crack, as if someone had been pressing outwards from beneath her skin.

In another girl, her bun held in place by a

pencil, I saw garland cracks, small short curves disrupting the marginal areas of her face like tiny waves. In the guy next to her, whose glasses could have used a good cleaning, a grid crack divided his high forehead into right angles that ran into each other, creating little irregular boxes.

The longer I applied what I'd just heard to the living specimens around me, imagining more and more fissures in their façades, the louder these fantasies of decomposition started to gather force, like a creature that after years of slumber at the bottom of the ocean in blackish-blue darkness is nudged by a current initiated somewhere far off, possibly by a small boat skimming the surface of the water leagues overhead, and, awakened, opens an enormous eye and prepares for the next voyage.

★   ★   ★

Yet at home my miniature landscapes seemed immune to the passage of time, as if in possession of a secret formula against erosion. The moths I'd replace every couple of months but the habitats themselves hardly needed upkeep apart from some careful dusting, and I began to long for high-viscosity magma to burst through the surface of the volcano, up through the crust to force open a new path.

* * *

Once my model of the excavation was nearly complete, layers of time set in sand and superglue, I decided I would try to depict geological stages in a different way. I would replicate Pegwell Bay, but without the boy or his relatives.

After some deliberation as to how to reproduce the cliffs I found a slice of plywood, the sort used at rock-climbing centres, and coated it with non-reflective varnish to give it the illusion of age. For the shallow inlet I used a layer of dull yellow packing paper, and added a few glints of reflected sunlight with a paintbrush. Last I grafted on the sunset, the sky a sheet of carton smudged with raw umber. But the paper I'd used for the inlet wasn't right, it wasn't the proper tone and didn't evoke anything, least of all an inlet on the south-eastern coast of England, so I tore it off in one go, taking along some of the rock since it had all been attached with superglue.

Over the next few days I brainstormed about what material I could use instead, what kind of paper or carton would capture the

151

still yet not entirely flat or smooth sheet of water from which the limestone boulders emerged, a simple task yet for some reason I couldn't think of the right material. A visit to Cass Art yielded nothing, nor a quick look in a crafts book in our museum shop. I would have to be extravagant and pay a visit to L. Cornelissen & Son in Great Russell Street.

This shop was always full of wonders: tall glass bottles of varnish, pigment and resin; apothecary jars filled with dry paint like sands from mythic beaches: Red Ochre and Manganese Blue, Cobalt Turquoise and Lapis Lazuli, Yellow Ochre and Egyptian Blue; reed pens and genuine Egyptian papyrus in case one of the mummies at the British Museum awakened with a thought; cigar-shaped pastels and labelled crayons; handmade paintbrushes the size of sceptres . . . After half an hour of gazing, during which I handled and considered and admired far more than I bought, I found a thin sheet of gold leaf perfect for the shallow inlet.

★   ★   ★

That night I came upon Jane and Lucian huddled close at the kitchen table, a pot of tea and an ashtray between them. Have a seat, Jane said, laughing nervously. I obliged.

Lucian rolled three cigarettes, playing with the strands of tobacco before fitting them into the paper. Out of courtesy I smoked one. Jane got up and poured me a cup of tea, then asked about my week. I muttered something about Daniel at the Tate and my visit to Cornelissen's. Lucian told me he'd sold fourteen skull rings to a group of Mexican kids in Misfits and Throbbing Gristle T-shirts. Jane told me about Funestre, a new band she'd signed. I sensed the issue of Lucian's past had been resolved. And that they hadn't spoken about the apparition on the balcony, or, if they had, Lucian hadn't got the full measure of what had happened. But then again, neither had I.

I finished my tea and stood up. Lucian offered to roll me another cigarette. Jane invited me to a gig that Wednesday. No thank you, I said to both, and wished them goodnight.

In my room, door closed and at my desk, I could hear her laughter in the kitchen, gleeful but tense, and smell the smoke from Lucian's cigarettes. Very gently I pressed my thumbs down on the gold leaf not wanting to tear it, gently gently till the surface became rippled, like a gilt shimmer on water capturing the last of the day's sun in the low tide, clinging to those last bits of illumination.

10

As much as Daniel and I tried to lose ourselves in our collections, it was hard to ignore the transition from late autumn to early winter, the shifts in colour and foliage outside and the swell in numbers within. Tourist season had begun and Christmas travellers were starting to flock to our museums and with them new languages, wider than the usual repertoire, began to float through the rooms. Yet beyond those walls the days grew darker and shorter, and expressions more sullen, as a steely melancholy bit into the city.

Over the past few weeks Daniel had been working on a new collection, *The Tinnitus of the Old Astronaut*, which gave rise to new hopes. The handful of correspondents to whom he'd sent samples commented on the great progress he had made, and the air of dignified resignation, as they called it, of his characters, all individuals who found themselves in the twilight of their careers: the old acrobat retired to the wings, the signalman losing his sight, the dancer with a shattered ankle, the porn star with disfigured breasts, the diabetic carpenter, forty kilos overweight, straining to lift his toolbox.

It wasn't old age that had inspired the poems, since Daniel was barely circling his mid-forties, but rather a deep weariness with regard to his own body, he said, the body he could never escape. This sense of entrapment was felt most in his limp, with which he just longed to part ways and cast off in some foreign city after dusk, but no, it was as loyal and resilient as a dog.

At least the acrobat, the astronaut, and even the porn star, he said, had been able to escape their own bodies and, for a few moments, flee their condition and enter something more hypnotic, but he had never had that, not even through his writing, for as he sat at his desk that hideous thing was still clutching at his foot and if it clutched at his foot it clutched at his mind, and he never felt entirely free. For years he had suffered the vertigo of existence, he said, but without experiencing any of its physical thrills. Even the damn contraption nailed to his living-room floor had become a problem, its sturdy wooden foot mocking him each time he walked past.

As opposed to his other poems, for which he required total silence, Daniel wrote the ones in this collection while listening over and over again to a favourite song from his youth, 'Death of a Clown', and it wasn't long before the graphic designer next door was driven mad and slipped two notes in his letterbox saying that if he must have something on repeat could he at least vary it weekly, or from time to time choose another Kinks song, but he just didn't understand, Daniel said, that no other song would conjure up the atmosphere required to finish his collection, and it wasn't only the lyrics — the dry, clagging make-up, the old fortune-teller lying dead on the floor, the insect trainer searching for his runaway fleas, the tigers that no longer roared — but the tune. And he couldn't listen to it through his headphones, either, for the funerary circus melody, or what he thought of as a funerary circus melody with its dying tambourine, had to be strung up, black and rattling, through his flat.

Like leaves unfastening from their tree, one by one he would print out each finished poem, a tiny obituary, and send it off.

* * *

To my surprise, for we had never taken a trip together despite our many years of friendship, Daniel asked me one evening whether I would like to go to Paris with him for the holidays. A correspondent of his, he explained, a poet from Ljubljana, was getting divorced from his wife of twelve years, and while they sorted things out in Slovenia their flat in Paris, where they had been living during their entire marriage, would remain empty. They weren't interested in making a profit at a time like this, he added, so all we'd have to pay for was food and the Eurostar.

I could feel the little hairs on my arms rising as I listened to his proposition. A holiday from Jane, from the flat, from the museum. Not to mention that the years came and went and I had rarely used my days off work for anything memorable; I'd remain in the city and simply sleep late, wander the streets, tinker with my landscapes, but after four or five days feel desperate for routine. And then there was the fact I would probably never in my life have the money to pay for two weeks in Paris myself. I had visited the city once, aged fifteen, and the memories were dim. The more I reflected, the more it seemed like a brilliant idea. I nearly interrupted Daniel with an immediate yes but caught the word just in time, remembering there were a few other factors to consider. I promised him an answer in a day or two.

True, he had been my best friend for the

past nine years. But I had never seen him first thing in the morning or last thing at night. We had never played house or even spent long unbroken spells of time together. There had always been an exit. I didn't want to introduce any complications. When I'd asked how many bedrooms he said he was *pretty sure* there were two. But what if there weren't?

All morning and afternoon at work, I debated. Like a dog that scratches at the door to be let in, and once inside it scratches at the door to be let out, and once you let it out all it wants is to enter again, and once you get up and open the door it comes in as if for the first time, only to change its mind seconds later and scratch at the door, which since it is winter must remain closed.

★   ★   ★

Some individuals, regardless of age, reach out and seize what they want from life. Others do not. The following day at work I witnessed the familiar dance between an old man and an empty chair. I had seen it many times. I was standing a few feet away quietly chatting with a colleague while trying, in the subtlest of ways, to assert my territory, when a white-haired man resembling an ancient mouse entered the room and immediately eyed my empty chair. He stared at it longingly but I could see him hesitate. At any moment I might return. He looked at me, then back at the chair. At me, back at the chair. After a minute or two he sighed and shuffled off into the next room to stare at the next empty chair he wouldn't occupy. I could have taken him by the arm and led him to one of the wooden benches in the other rooms. Or told him that, despite having the best paintings, the Sainsbury Wing had the least comfortable chairs.

★ ★ ★

After a dozen mental back-and-forths, I accepted. Daniel immediately wrote to his friend to make arrangements.

★ ★ ★

'What do you mean you're going away for two weeks?'

The moment of most overlap in our lives, if I stayed up late enough, took place in the kitchen over a pot of tea. Jane flicked the switch on the kettle and reached for a pack of blue Pall Malls on the counter. Since Lucian, she had started smoking again full-time.

'I have a chance to go to Paris, for free.'

'We were going to repaint the flat.'

'We can do it the first weekend I'm back.'

She waved her hand. 'Don't bother. I'll do it myself. January's going to be a really busy month at work. I won't have time and I want to start the year with nice white walls.'

She bent over the stove and lit a cigarette, then tilted her head as she exhaled loudly for effect.

'What about Lucian? Can't he help?'

'He's going up north to see his brother. Basically I'm going to be here on my jacksy for two bloody weeks.'

'I'm sorry Jane, but it's too good to turn down. Daniel is being lent a flat.'

'Are you going to be sharing a bedroom?'

I had to snuff out the glint in her eye, quick. 'Of course not.'

'Well, there might be a bit of night migration.'

'No, there won't, trust me.'

My flatmate and best friend had met only a handful of times, and on those few occasions neither had made much of an effort. In Daniel's eyes, Jane was 'relentlessly morose'. In Jane's eyes, Daniel was distant and pretentious. When thrown into the same space, Daniel always asked about any new bands she'd signed, and Jane would ask how

160

his writing was going, and from there the conversation would grind to an awkward halt unless I came to the rescue.

'You wait and see.' She raised an eyebrow and laughed, a hoarse, dusky laugh I'd never heard coming out of her before.

11

Daniel told me to envision the Eurostar as a giantess straddling two cities. London lay at her ankles, Paris at her head, and as the train hurtled through towns, fields and somewhat lacklustre landscape, we were moving up her thighs, he said, circling the curve of her waist, sloping up and across her breasts, and would finally emerge on her face, a mechanical murmur pressing down on her lips, the slant of her nose, her sea of hair.

In the four-seat configuration we each had a window, the third seat was empty, and in the fourth sat a Chinese man who spent the journey underlining passages in a Bible with red and green markers. At one point the train slipped into a tunnel and we crossed the inside of the giantess, history smoothed out into twenty minutes of subterranean darkness, a diplomatic handshake 150 feet underwater. The black outside the window was severed in two by the blur of the rail, and for a few moments I forgot our destination.

Once we emerged from the tunnel and into France the landscape went from barren to populated within minutes, as if an animator were feverishly working to fill in the space. The train zoomed past rows of wind turbines, three-pronged ghosts slicing the air, and pylons that looked like metal cat's cradle or some other thread-pulling game. Rows of dour apartment blocks, the next thing to jab the horizon, sprang into view as the rural landscape receded. Paris was coming into focus.

★ ★ ★

The poet from Ljubljana had sent Daniel detailed instructions on how to reach his flat from the Gare du Nord. After a brief ride on the RER we emerged at the Luxembourg Gardens and wheeled our suitcases noisily along the uneven streets, past busy cafés and dusk-filled corners until reaching rue Claude Bernard, then down its sloping pavement to number 49. The entrance was marked by large green doors so heavy they required two hands to push open and beyond these doors stood the bird-like concierge, who after confirming our identity handed us the keys and explained something to Daniel while pointing towards the courtyard. We crossed this courtyard, climbed a flight of stairs, then another.

The flat smelled of gunpowder and

candyfloss, as if a clown had just departed. I let Daniel go in first, then stepped out from behind him and began to survey. At the centre of the room stood a bulbless lamp on a stand. Evening entered through a vertical tear in one of the curtains. A small chair faced into a corner. I imagined a semi-empty theatre months after its last performance, the props now obsolete, the final act played out long ago, the actors involved in other productions, their lines from the old play forgotten and replaced by newer, more relevant ones.

All around us lay the remnants of someone else's life. Unwatered plants, decomposing flies on the sills, unwashed plates in the sink, crumpled linen in the hamper, clumps of dust and hair on nearly every surface. A corridor linked the rooms in railway-car configuration: bedroom, living room, kitchen, bedroom, bathroom. Like an estranged married couple I gravitated towards the larger bedroom and Daniel took the smaller one, presumably for guests. The living room faced the street, the other rooms, the interior courtyard. There were no photographs anywhere and during our entire stay I was to keep revising my image of the ill-fated couple, hard to gauge from the few items they left in the wardrobe, a dark plum woollen man's suit and a black chiffon dress with oversized white cuffs. In the bathroom by the sink lay a brush full of long strands of greyish blonde hair.

Daniel instantly laid claim to the writing desk in the living room and moved it to face the window. Before unpacking his clothes he prepared his workplace. Books, papers, folders, a mug from the kitchen for his pens. Though nothing was said, it was understood I would never go near the area.

The fridge contained half a block of butter, a bottle of white wine and a jar of expired mayonnaise. We had a late dinner at an Italian across the street, an excellent place the poet from Ljubljana had recommended in a footnote. Along with our pizzas Daniel ordered a carafe of house red, and with every glass we clinked to two weeks away from our collections and routines, apart from his writing. The evening was buoyed by a lightness we'd rarely felt and we rounded it off by ordering two panna cottas and a second carafe.

We returned to the flat by ten, Daniel almost timid as he turned the key in the door, and after a slightly awkward goodnight in the living room that was different from all our goodnights in London, we said *See you at breakfast* and headed to our respective rooms.

Exhausted from the journey and slightly

giddy from the wine, I slipped on a T-shirt and pyjama bottoms, washed in the bathroom once Daniel had had his turn, and brought a glass of water to my bedside. With the lamp off and the curtains firmly closed, a welcome darkness spilled over the room.

Yet almost immediately this darkness began to curdle into something viscous and heavy. As I lay in bed I began to speculate about the couple who'd slept in my spot for who knows how many years. I tried to imagine their faces, their bodies, their voices, whether they slept on their sides, stomachs or backs, whether intertwined or at separate ends of the bed, about whatever moments, fraught or transcendent, they'd lived out where I lay, what conversations, what passion or frustration. I began to worry I might inherit their dreams, that I'd find myself in ragged environments populated by ragged figures without knowing how to fend them off.

They'd certainly left behind a mood of unease, this couple, not necessarily imprinted on the mattress or pillows but rather on the stagnant air in the room, which lingered after I'd opened the windows. Even the set of sleep-courting images I had perfected in London over time — the paintings in the Gallery reduced to fuzzy squares and the night shifters, or night sifters, as we preferred

166

to call them, who watched over them; Roland's dentures in a glass by his bed, the submerged ruins of an ancient city; the moths on Jane's strips, struggling for take-off — not even this brief sequence of images, which I'd run through whenever I had trouble falling asleep, worked to counter the others that night.

And how strange to imagine Daniel in the room down the corridor, asleep or awake, doing what, who knew, but it felt odd to be geographically close at this late hour with nothing but two doors between us. I began to regret having chosen the larger bedroom, fantasising now about a narrower bed, one with less history perhaps, and a room where the walls didn't extend so far out.

My mind felt more and more like an occupied lift travelling up and down the shaft of a building, never stopping at any floor to release its passengers, just continuing its purposeless journey until morning. To make matters worse, I became aware of a large television at the foot of the bed, its ominous square watching my every movement and non-movement. After half an hour of lying under its gaze I got up and wheeled it out into the corridor, where it remained for the rest of our stay. At around three I remembered Daniel's stash of sleeping pills and his offer to help myself should the need arise, so I stumbled to the bathroom and after rummaging through his toiletries bag found the bottle and helped myself to two temazepams. Why two, I wasn't sure, but ten milligrams hadn't seemed like enough. I slept late into the following day, emerging from my room at noon to find Daniel at his desk.

★　★　★

And then there was the world that lay beyond rue Claude Bernard. Once through the heavy green doors, we slowly opened ourselves up to the city. Daniel searched for hints of its past, for images unloosed from the verses of his favourite poets, the small draughts and currents, he called them, that had survived the nineteenth century and still blew through the streets. From arrondissement to arrondissement, without map or destination, he would stop to take notes while I in the meantime began to assemble my own little mental collage, plucking things from outside and placing them together in my head. In a foreign city ordinary sights acquire new meaning: a hidden cornice becomes a mysterious sign, a jowly man leaning out of his window becomes a medieval grotesque, the black Labrador leading a blind man becomes a shadow cast forward.

* * *

Before anything we agreed to visit the Louvre, so the next day, along with a herd of ashen-faced tourists, we descended into the land beneath the pyramid. Museum/ mausoleum, to me there was little difference; the people moving dumbly down the escalators looked like a procession of souls entering a vast sepulchre, and the further down we went, the stronger the taste of mouldy, ancient stone in my mouth.

Coats checked and tickets in hand, Daniel asked where I'd like to start. For its name I chose the Denon wing, which turned out to be an anthill. Wherever we went, whatever room we entered, we never seemed far from the drone of humanity, a drone I had never heard at the Gallery. It was as though people, afraid of silence, were filling up the space with talk. Every few rooms we'd pass a *plan de situation*, a map of the museum around which visitors huddled and pointed as if trying to figure out their place in the universe. Most rooms also contained *agents de surveillance*, unsmiling individuals, so different from us, who watched over the collection in elegant blue suits, much nicer than our mouse grey.

In the Salon Carré, a square room with Florentine paintings, I nearly forgot I wasn't in uniform when I saw a man pointing dangerously close to Giotto's St Francis of Assisi, a golden honeycomb of a work that depicted the saint feeding a flock of birds. I turned to look at the guard, sitting so still as if embalmed, but his attention was for some reason fixed on the ceiling.

The man's forefinger was definitely going beyond the six or seven inches permitted. He was pointing something out to his son, yet the boy paid no heed and gazed down at his shoes. Soon the finger was only a fraction of an inch from the Giotto, I couldn't believe my eyes, he was nearly *touching* the wooden panel, about to disturb over seven centuries of paint, a human intervention centimillideci-metres away, in fact he had probably already disturbed the paint surface, upset the membrane, changed the temperature. Why wasn't an alarm sounding? I could just imagine a spiral crack forming around the point of pressure, exactly where the finger pressed down, the extent of the damage not evident at first, until dust particles entered and accumulated over time, stealthily like a small draught in a chimney, pushing up and then through until a concentric pattern rose into sight.

To my surprise Daniel remained unperturbed, and assured me nothing would happen. Yet I stayed put until the irksome man had withdrawn his finger and walked off with his son.

Around the corner from the Giotto we came upon the *Battle of San Romano*, a far more unsettling version than ours at the Gallery. The figure at the centre had eyes like hollows and practically no nose. Together with its rearing black horse, they looked ready to plunge into the dark depths of the museum.

'Pure Uccello, master of illusion,' Daniel said, 'a man nearly driven mad by his quest for perspective.'

As we moved from room to room, stopping every now and then to half contemplate a portrait or landscape, Daniel told me about how this great painter had spent much of his life observing birds and beasts from every angle, reducing muscles and mass to fluid lines, so absorbed in his pursuit of perspective as he sat drawing for hours and hours in his modest house, that he forgot to feed himself as well as Selvaggia, the beautiful thirteen-year-old who had gone to live with him, noticing little more than the inflection lines in her face when she smiled feebly and the diminishing curves of her body, oblivious to the fact she was starving to death, and even once her limbs had gone stiff and she'd stopped blinking, he continued to draw her, still absorbed in his eternal search for the vanishing point.

After wandering through a couple of centuries of painting, Daniel led me to the oldest, coolest and quietest part of the museum. From the centre of the room rose the keep of an original twelfth-century chateau, the earliest foundations, a sign said, of the Louvre itself. We stepped onto a walkway suspended above what was once the moat and walked between walls of unhewn stone. It was easy to envision this section, with only four visitors and not a single guard, as the magical centre of the museum, everything balanced on its massive stone shoulders. The walkway girdled three quarters of the keep and then stopped, the last section unexcavated, an unambiguous punctuation mark, and only in this room was I able to relax a little.

★ ★ ★

'Did Uccello really ignore his girlfriend to the extent she starved to death?' I asked at dinner that night.

'That's what they say.'

172

'But he loved her?'

'To him she was a marvel of lines, circles and curves.'

I couldn't help wondering whether Daniel — if he and I ever had been together — would've, in his obsessions, been capable of letting me starve, there in a foreign city where no one would know, as I turned brittle and then stiff in a chair while he scribbled away at his desk.

★   ★   ★

It was mostly at night that I thought about the troubled couple whose home we were occupying. During the day it was easy to block them out, and I sensed Daniel did too, yet how could we not think of them when thrown into this daily intimacy we'd never experienced in London, even the simple fact of breakfast had to be dealt with, starting the day face to face, and then the question of the bathroom, our toothbrushes side by side, towels too, the leftover moisture from his bath settling into mine.

★   ★   ★

The next morning, after a strong cup of coffee, I left Daniel at his desk — it made me uncomfortable to see him at work, as if I were coming too close to the act of creation — and set out in a black trilby I had found in the wardrobe. Despite taking the small streets I arrived, in that mysterious tropism one has towards big avenues, at boulevard Saint-Germain. I found a place selling sandwiches, bought one, then searched for a place to eat. I passed several benches, most of them unoccupied, but was deterred by the streams of people, assertive tourists and meandering locals, or perhaps meandering tourists and assertive locals.

Fortunately I didn't have to look long. Across the street, beside the church of Saint-Germain, I discovered a green intermission: a small triangular park containing tall trees, a bronze head on a pedestal surrounded by pigeons, and a scattering of individuals eating their lunch on benches. The place surpassed my expectations. Yet just as I was stepping through the gate I caught sight, in a corner at the far end and half hidden by a tree, of the back of a *clochard* peeing in the bushes. I stopped and stared, half fascinated, I admit, by the snag in an otherwise bucolic scene. No one else seemed to notice him or, if they did, no one cared. But I realised I could no longer join them, my decision somehow reinforced by a metal sign in tennis-court green attached to the gate, *EN CAS DE TEMPÊTE CE JARDIN SERA FERMÉ*. In case of tempest this garden will close, I gathered in my creaky school French, as I ran my fingertips along the smooth border.

In the end I ate while I walked, hardly ideal but I was too timid to sit down somewhere and eat on my own, captive to that irrational behaviour common in foreign cities when you feel everyone is watching when in reality not a soul has noticed your existence. Later that afternoon as I wandered along the Seine an unpleasant sleet began to fall. I would have gone home but didn't want to interrupt Daniel, who was probably still at work. Yet I also wanted to avoid the anxiety of museums and the awkwardness of entering shops where I knew I wouldn't buy anything.

I continued onwards, turning into streets at random, the foreignness of the city condensed that day into the curious pods I saw fastened to the walls abutting the river, large metal boxes closed with padlocks, perched in rows like cocoons, and I wondered whether they were lockers for bathers or closed puppet theatres or storage facilities for students before realising they were *bouquiniste* stalls once the *bouquinistes* had gone home, the bookshops folded into themselves, their cellophane-wrapped inventories shielded

175

from both dusk and rain.

Daniel and I had stopped once or twice to admire the hanging prints that danced along the cords on windy days, reanimated images of extinct scenes, and all the other flapping inventory pinned down by heavy stones, and I'd even spotted a reproduction of something from our Gallery, a faded traveller whose palette had been drained in another climate, and my heart had skipped a beat.

*　*　*

Over dinner we compared notes. I described my day and Daniel told me how after writing all morning he'd set out late in the afternoon to catch the last snatches of daylight and ended up at Stern, the venerable old stationers in the Passage des Panoramas. But when he arrived the shop was not only closed but entirely empty. There was no one inside yet all the lights were on, the chandeliers casting a glow over the elegant furniture — carved chairs with green upholstery and matching tables, vertical oak shelves, bureaus with glass doors, a paradise of polished wooden floors and panelling.

Lit desk lamps shone onto vacant surfaces, chairs gathered round tables at imaginary meetings, you could almost see the echo of a face in the mirror above the marble mantelpiece flanked by caryatids. He imagined a company of shadows going about its work, shelving papers, customising letterheads, guillotining paper in two with a stroke.

Never had such elegance, and so much polished wood, looked so ghostly. In one window was a small plaque that read 'Stern Medaille d'Or 1867'. In the next window, a large sign with a telephone number. In the third, a thick black curtain like those in funeral parlours. In fact, not only the stationers but much of the passage felt forsaken, and its ancient skylights gave it a tired aquatic glow. That's the strange thing about Paris, Daniel concluded, you go in search of its vestigial glory, seeking traces here and there, but apart from the occasional current, the past denies you entry, and so it was that despite all the illumination, the doors of Stern remained closed.

★　★　★

I was already in bed with the lights out when I heard the brass handle of the door to my room being pressed down and, seconds later, a push. Light entered from the corridor and Daniel's silhouette came into view. He whispered my name. I didn't answer. He said it again, a bit louder, wavering in the doorway. I couldn't tell whether he could see my eyes were half open or whether he assumed I was asleep. We'd said goodnight only ten minutes before. My arm itched all of a sudden but I resisted lifting a hand to scratch it, remaining as still as I could. It was the way he'd said my name.

He didn't persist. After a few more seconds at the threshold he withdrew, pulling the door closed ever so gently behind him. I considered calling him back. Of course I had thought many times of what it would be like. And I'd always been drawn to his mouth, the bee-stung lips, often chapped, and the small gap between his front teeth. After all, we were in another city, in other beds, under someone else's roof, now would be the moment, more than any other, to try something new.

But no, to summon him would be too much of a risk, I reminded myself, and as I listened to his irregular steps retreating down the corridor I slipped further under the covers, processing what had just happened, namely, that my best friend had tried, for whatever reason, to step over the silent and invisible boundary we had drawn long ago, almost as soon as we'd met, the boundary that had held our friendship in such perfect place. Together we had composed our hymn to distance, that magical distance that held the best of life in place. *The music of the night*, Daniel once quoted, *lies not in the stars but in the darkness between them.* And yet that evening, perhaps driven by nothing more than an impulse or curiosity, he had attempted to redraw the line, which may have been glorious or disastrous depending on the results, but I didn't want to risk it, no, and as I lay there trying to sleep in the doomed couple's bed, positioned at the centre in order to not be fully on his side or hers, I began to worry about a new imbalance, the kind that might arise from a small shift, when a tiny peg is removed from one hole and inserted in another.

★　★　★

'Coffee or tea?' he asked when I entered the kitchen at half past ten. I'd lain in bed an extra hour, hoping that perhaps I would find him at his desk by the time I came out for breakfast.

'Tea's fine,' I said, reaching for the pot. He reached for it at the same time. Our hands met. Mine quickly withdrew.

He poured me a mug and turned back to his toast.

'How'd you sleep?'

'Fine,' I lied. 'And you?'

'Like a dead man.'

I felt his eyes on me as I opened the jar of honey, so delicious it tasted of forest, and spooned some onto my plate.

'The bread's still warm,' he said, passing me the basket.

'Thanks.'

'I was thinking . . . '

He paused. I bit into my toast, dreading the end of the sentence, and stared down at the ugly vinyl tablecloth.

' . . . that we could go to the menagerie today, at the Jardin des Plantes. Have you ever been there?'

I shook my head.

'It's one of the oldest zoos in the world. I'd like to go. I have some poems in mind.'

'Sure,' I said, eager for some activity and distraction, and relieved that last night's visitation had gone unmentioned.

★　★　★

A gravel path led us through a sweep of manicured gardens, past rows of thorny hedges and denuded trees, past the seated statue of Buffon, the great naturalist under whose direction the zoo had flourished. It led us past a large rotunda of vaulted green iron

180

and glass reminiscent of a train station, past countless signs in assorted typefaces, their edges darkened by rust, and, finally, to the menagerie itself.

The first animals to arrive in 1793, our pamphlet said, were saved from the king's private zoo at Versailles, pillaged during the Terror. Many, including a camel, had already been eaten or destroyed. In 1795 France acquired its first elephant and in 1827 its first giraffe (a present to Charles X from the pasha of Egypt), inspiring a craze that featured everything from songs, poems and vignettes to gingerbread giraffes and 'coiffure à la girafe', high chignons held aloft by a wire frame.

The first animals we stopped to admire seemed entirely removed from, in fact almost resistant to, this animated past: a giant tortoise in its domed brown carapace resting alongside a rock of equal size, the two locked in a contest of immobility, and a lone black yak dozing on the dirt ground of its enclosure, its eyes half closed and front legs tucked under, its shabby coat like a worn blanket, L-shaped horns pointed upwards as if waiting for signals from a mountaintop continents away. A pair of majestic eagle owls, or *hiboux grand duc*, seated on high branches like small, sad kings. Placid dromedaries with faded patches on their knees.

Daniel began to say something but I moved away, desiring silence while I looked, and motioned to him before stepping into the vivarium. Inside, three stock-still Nile crocodiles suspended in shallow water like strips of bark, a snake with an unblinking silver eye like a coin, a leaf-green chameleon on a branch basking in the ersatz glow of a sunlamp. A few paces behind, Daniel had followed me in, and once near he remarked on the effective camouflage of some of the reptiles, almost lost to the eye in their viridescent surroundings, too long a word for too simple a thought, and then fell silent. The stuffy air of the vivarium was only tolerable for a short while. After five minutes we emerged and took a path to our right that led us to the monkey section, where large skittish eyes hung over pairs of little black hands clasping the wire nettings.

The great aviary was filled with diurnal birds of prey, all kinds of landscapes of feathers inside, some moving and others very still. The only free birds we saw were a gang of pigeons loitering beneath, pecking at some fallen seed; even birds must understand that beauty has a price. Daniel began jotting something down in his notebook. Standing with his legs anchored apart, he looked up every now and then at the trapped brush-strokes beyond the bars, strokes thicker than the ones we were used to, and back down at his writing. If I didn't know, I'd think he was sketching the birds rather than finding words for them.

As the afternoon started to thicken, his figure, especially when hunched over his notebook that way, took on a somewhat sinister aspect, much less attractive than any of the creatures around us, and I started to feel slightly annoyed too by the unevenness of his gait. In fact that day his limp, at such variance with his other movements, rattled me to such an extent I found myself silently, guiltily, willing him a headache. Anything to remove the limp: bring back the Hungarian and resummon, reconjure, resurrect the headache, I thought to myself as we walked more or less side by side, and at first I thought he'd read my mind when he quoted a poem about a caged panther forever pacing round one centre, its mighty will paralysed, its vision wearied by the bars.

As if in answer to this sudden burst of quotation, we arrived at the snow leopard. Judging from the enraptured crowds circling the enclosure this animal was the zoo's main attraction. People held up their children, murmured and exclaimed, snapped dozens of pictures. The metallic light at that hour, a bluish silver, made the cat look even more powerful and mysterious, and before long I too succumbed to its spell, transfixed by the glacial green eyes flecked with sparks of boredom and irritation, pride and captivity impossible partners, and the fluid, elegant movements of the large spotted paws. It was the only creature that day that looked straight back at us, silently hissing — ears pinned back and jaws sprung open — and for a heart-stopping second I forgot there was a pane of glass between us.

Dusk fell at four thirty — from elsewhere, a loud squawking of parrots — and we followed the painted wooden exit signs and passed through the turnstile. On the way home, Daniel stopped several times to write in his notebook and answered in monosyllables when I asked what we were having for dinner or doing tomorrow. That afternoon there could've been a glass pane and two rows of bars between us; perhaps I had imagined his voice and the open door.

★ ★ ★

And then, that very night, he arrived. At half past ten, in a dark blue suit. Daniel was at his desk and I was heading to the kitchen for something sweet when the outside buzzer rang. We looked at one another, puzzled. We weren't expecting anyone. From the window facing the street, we saw the figure of a man paying a taxi. On the pavement beside him, a suitcase and a briefcase. The taxi drove off. The man dragged his luggage over to the door. He was no longer visible from where we stood.

The buzzer rang a second time.

Minutes later, the bell to our flat. Someone, possibly the concierge, had let the man into the building and he was now right outside. Our doorbell again. I followed Daniel as he went to investigate. He peered through the peephole, shrugged in response to whatever he saw, and opened.

Outside stood a slender man with bags under his eyes and a white, heart-shaped face. He wore a suit and shiny brown shoes and his dark hair was combed into a side parting with each section slicked down, the furrows of the comb still visible. Early to mid-fifties I would say, though it was hard to tell.

'Gregor?' the man said.

'No, he's in Ljubljana.'

The man looked surprised. He rubbed his forehead and craned his neck to look past us, as if checking to see whether Daniel was telling the truth.

'He's not here. Can I take a message?'

'My name is Pierre,' the man said forlornly. 'From Stockholm. I expect Gregor.'

Daniel's face lit up. 'Pierre Zekeli?'

The man nodded.

And our trip slipped away.

'Well, I am Daniel, Daniel Harper, from London.'

More astonishment.

'The poet?'

'Yes!'

At this word, Pierre lunged forward and threw his arms around him, the seams of his suit nearly bursting, the smell of pine cologne rising off his clothes.

'Come in, my friend,' Daniel said, and helped him with his suitcase.

I closed the door and followed.

Pierre scanned the living room as he walked in, his eyes resting for a moment on Daniel's busy desk. After setting down his briefcase he excused himself and headed towards the bathroom, and on his way back detoured into the kitchen for a glass of water. He was clearly familiar with the place.

'Daniel Harper,' Pierre muttered to himself in a funny accent, smiling.

I cleared my throat and held out a hand.

'And I'm Marie.'

'Oh yes, this is Marie,' Daniel echoed.

Pierre shook my hand with his cold one.

'But where is Gregor?' he asked Daniel.

'Gregor's in Ljubljana.'

'Why?'

'He's getting divorced.'

The smile disappeared. 'From Barbara?'

Pierre went to the sofa and steadied himself on an armrest.

'But they were together since sixteen.'

'Well, that's probably why.'

In order to lighten the news, Daniel went to the kitchen and returned with a good bottle of whisky we'd bought at the shop on the corner.

After knocking back a tumbler, Pierre asked for three hangers. He opened his scuffed leather suitcase, a fine make and well travelled, and hung three dark blue suits like the one he was wearing in the closet by the door. That was the most he would ever unpack.

Daniel asked whether he was hungry.

No, Pierre replied, the only thing he required was an ashtray.

Once a saucer had been provided (we couldn't find an ashtray despite our guest insisting Gregor was a heavy smoker himself) Pierre poured himself another tumbler and produced a dented cigarette case embossed with two griffins from his jacket pocket. He lit his cigarette with a match. Once he'd taken a few puffs, inhaling deeply as if savouring every particle, he turned to Daniel and asked whether he knew anything more about the divorce.

No, Daniel said, he knew nothing, in fact he had never met Gregor; the particulars of his life were unknown to him, apart from what he happened to mention in letters.

Pierre topped up his tumbler, turned the bottle towards him to study the label. His nails were manicured and he wore a gold ring with some kind of emblem on his little finger.

Once Daniel had poured out two more tumblers for us, we all sat down at the kitchen table, by then the designated focal point of the flat, and over the next two hours, over a litany of questions and answers — how was so-and-so, had Daniel seen the latest anthology of French and Czech poetry, or the Finnish journal with the piece on Celan, and many other things I couldn't possibly relate to — Pierre finished off our twelve-year-old Johnnie Walker. I watched as the bottle's coppery contents sank from three quarters to half full to a quarter to empty.

With the last remaining drops, to which he added an inch of tap water, Pierre swallowed three pills, two pink and one white, which he extracted from his briefcase, kept at his feet at all times like a small, obedient dog. Within minutes of ingesting them, his head began to droop and his cigarette started missing the saucer, small mounds of ash accumulating on the table.

Just as his eyes were closing like the shutters of a bookshop, Daniel showed him the sofa. He offered to make it into a bed but in a last flourish of energy Pierre raised his hand and said he liked sleeping on hard surfaces.

And there he slept, for eighteen hours. As far as I could tell, he didn't even get up once to use the bathroom. Don't worry about him, Daniel would say each time he caught me looking over. Are you sure he's fine? I would ask, to which Daniel would answer, Of course. He'll wake up when he recovers from his trip. But Sweden's not that far away, I'd say, to which Daniel would reply, somewhat enigmatically, *Depends how you measure distances*.

★   ★   ★

As it turned out, Pierre spent half his visit asleep. Even when awake, he seemed in a permanent state of tilting into sleep, and when asleep he continued to look impeccable, his face as smooth as his hair,

189

everything in place, elegant and unruffled. In many ways, he was the perfect guest.

He didn't cost us much either, since he barely ate. At dinner he would take a few polite bites, fork always in left hand, knife in right, and discreetly push the unwanted food to one side of his plate. He'd then rise from his chair and walk over to the bookcase to fetch the saucer, sit down again and smoke through the rest of the meal. I knew Daniel disliked eating amidst fumes but he never protested, instead listening attentively as Pierre spoke to him about poems he had written, 'L'après-midi d'une nuance' and 'Pour en faire de grands parkings', and how the lukewarm reception of these early attempts in French had made him turn full-time to translation, although at the back of his mind he still harboured plans to write '*le poème total*'.

Every now and then Daniel would turn to check on me, but mainly his attention was riveted on his friend. Pierre's English was bizarre, an invention seemingly his own, unlike the English of Scandinavian or Eastern European visitors to our Gallery whose origins were betrayed as soon as they came up to ask a question. When I commented on Pierre's use of the word catarrh (he'd arrived with a mild cold) Daniel leapt to remind me

190

that English was his *fifth* language, after Romanian, Swedish, French and German.

Towards the end of dinner, or, rather, as Daniel and I were finishing ours, Pierre would wash down a few pills with his wine and half an hour later, like clockwork, crumple into his chair. Sometimes we would leave him in this position, which looked far from comfortable, but usually Daniel would slip his hands under his armpits and drag his friend to the sofa and stretch him out horizontal, then remove his shoes and place them by the briefcase at his feet.

★　★　★

Lying there, just *lying there*. And yet, from the moment he appeared to the moment he departed, Pierre exerted his influence. How could it be that someone who spent most of his time immobile could have such a strong hold on my friend? From good morning to good night, Daniel was in some kind of a trance. It didn't matter whether Pierre was awake or asleep or, as it appeared most of the time, somewhere in between. Was the temperature in the living room warm enough, Daniel wondered, or should he turn up the heating? Would the sound of the coffee grinder wake him, or the toaster's chime?

Afternoons, Pierre tended to awaken as if by some inner alarm clock. From one second to the next the unwound toy on our sofa would start to move and sit up, and Daniel would rush over to offer him coffee, which he would down like a shot of whisky. After Pierre bathed, another activity he relished judging by the time it took him, they would slip on their coats and set out. Daniel would ask whether I wanted to come along. Half of me wanted to say yes, but then I'd imagine walking alongside them while they discussed their business, every now and then turning, out of belated courtesy, to ask me a question, and I decided I'd rather be on my own. Well, what did I expect; the balance of a ship is always tipped when someone new comes onboard.

And so I did what I had always done best. I stood back and observed, withdrew into the quiet, neutral zone that felt comfortably familiar, registering voices and movements without interfering.

Yet as the days wore on, that long, smooth expanse of patience began to curl up at the edges. Often I'd leave the two men to their hermitage and go for walks on my own. I spent an inordinate amount of time window-shopping and came to know the ornaments and mannequins in the shopfronts near us quite well, imagining a secret dialogue between the shiny black marble of the local undertakers, the bright red machines at the twenty-four-hour laundrette and the pouting plastic heads in the wig shop. I also walked further, through lavish gardens and humbler squares, down imposing avenues and narrow streets full of stalls, and entered every church I passed to warm myself for a few minutes.

Pierre stole six days from our twelve in Paris, large black Xs in the calendar. He turned Daniel's attention away from me and I found myself wanting it back. Christmas came and went, or maybe it was New Year's, in any case, a night like any other apart from what our guest contributed to dinner, four bottles of wine with fancy labels and a bag of white-capped gingerbread biscuits he must have found at a shop on rue Mouffetard unless he brought them from Sweden. We lit candles, worked our way through a chestnut casserole, then spent two hours tidying up while Pierre sat pensively on the sofa, saucer balanced on knee, smoking one cigarette after the other.

★ ★ ★

Late one morning when Daniel was out I decided to vacuum the flat. We had yet to do any cleaning and I'd begun noticing large dustballs in the corners that floated up whenever someone walked past. If I didn't clean, no one would. I made my way down the corridor to the living room where Pierre lay asleep on the sofa. At first I avoided the area but after cleaning all around it, including the invisible moat encircling Daniel's desk, I slowly advanced towards Pierre, noticing a few especially large clumps of dust by his briefcase. Despite the machine's loud rumble he didn't stir.

Once I finished, I returned the vacuum cleaner to the cupboard and went to have another look at Pierre. It was fascinating to see how profoundly he slept. I had never witnessed such deep sleep in my life, a sleep that seemed to block out the present so determinedly, it was hard to know in what time zone he existed.

My eyes fell on the briefcase. There it sat, just waiting to be opened and inspected. Tiny screaming devils jumped up and down in my head and, despite never having trespassed in my life, I couldn't help but listen. The latches made a snapping sound. Pierre didn't react. My fingers trembled as I lifted the lid.

Yet inside I found no secrets, at least as far as I could tell, only a small, personal arsenal for survival: eight opaque medicine bottles with labels in Swedish, two bundles of addressed envelopes from foreign lands, three felt-tipped pens, a couple of books in French by strange-looking characters named Michaux and Daumal, a thick leather address book with loose pages, six bags of liquorice coins, and a red plastic comb with two missing teeth.

Pierre mumbled something behind me. I jumped up and turned. His eyes were still closed, he was in the exact same position as before. I quickly relatched the briefcase and returned it to its place. Pierre mumbled again, something like turkey gurgling in various languages, a kind of sleep-talking Esperanto, and I took it as a warning, issued from beyond, to stop prying.

I hurried away just in time. Daniel was at the door, key turning in lock.

★ ★ ★

The following morning I rose to discover the men had gone out. Alone, I cast my eyes around the flat and after a full wander was gripped by an overwhelming magnetism, as if someone had thrown a lasso round my waist and was pulling me, towards Daniel's desk. Until then it had been silently and unconditionally off limits but now, as the day before, I felt entitled to explore.

The desk gave off an aromatic wooden smell as if the drawers were full of shavings. A few books in Slovenian lay piled in a corner beside a very smooth, very white stone that seemed to have come from the sea. Closer to the centre were Daniel's implements, a French-English dictionary and four other books, a stack of manila folders, the mug holding pencils and pens.

I picked up a lined page torn out from his notebook, from what I could decipher mostly scrawls about the snow leopard, and was wondering how it would look shredded into smaller pieces, half a word here, half a word there, when I was distracted by a book. Dozens of pages had been marked with strips of paper that emerged from the top and sides. What drew me to it wasn't the obsessive marking, however, which I'd often seen in books at Daniel's flat in London, but the cover. It was an explosion of white against black, like a self-combusting, dust-cloaked star: the ghostly spasm of a woman in a bed engulfed by the darkness of a room.

Intrigued, I drew the book closer, opening it to a random page. Upon seeing the first pictures I was so startled I almost took a step back. Inside, dozens of black and white photographs of somewhat savage women, much more intense than the women I'd been seeing on the street, rose to greet me. Most of them wore nightgowns or else fitted dresses or two-piece outfits that called to mind brothel residents from another era. They stood, sat or lay in bizarre positions, one with her back arched into a bridge, another swooning in a chair with her right leg stretched outwards and her wrist twisted anticlockwise. One woman stuck out her tongue to the left, another smiled dementedly into the distance. Another sat with folded arms and a crooked mouth while disembodied hands jabbed pins into her temples. Another had a face like an empty cage, her agitated hands like the birds that had flown away. Others stood in odd, rigid positions, their arms at ninety-degree angles to their trunks. In every picture there was something deviant, one body part that refused to conform, like branches rejecting the sun.

The text was in French but I didn't need language to read the faces and bodies lost in disorienting studio black. Unframed, the figures floated like dying stars at the centre of the page, or, pinned to a bed, like cosmic butterfly nebulae without the symmetry. As much as I tried, I couldn't understand who or what they were, what all this energy, white against black and body against bed, could mean.

I closed the book and went to take a shower, making the water hotter and hotter until I could bear it no longer. Yet right after drying off I went straight back to the book, desirous to continue. New faces rose to meet me, together with some I'd glimpsed earlier, and I began to feel similar to that restless matter, whatever it was, somehow trapped in the wrong casing. Several of the women looked into the camera seductively but others seemed to push away an invisible aggressor; I couldn't understand why they'd allowed themselves to be photographed.

★   ★   ★

The rest of the afternoon, squandered. I couldn't pull myself away. Over and over I thought of leaving the flat but would then pour myself another glass of water, make myself a sandwich, a cup of tea, then another, then another sandwich, more water. Every so often I returned to the living room and circled Daniel's desk, or rather, the book, half expecting something to drift up from its pages and free me. Finally, at a quarter to five, I forced myself to go for a walk but by then the sun had withdrawn so I stuck to familiar streets in the neighbourhood.

⋆　⋆　⋆

That evening Daniel decided to try out a recipe he recalled from his married years; dinner was pushed back an hour. While he rushed around the kitchen banging, clanging and dropping things, Pierre and I sat in front of the small black and white television whose surface was coated in a sticky layer of dust. Every now and then I got up to change the channel but found nothing I could understand, and Pierre didn't really seem to be watching. I considered turning up the volume all the way to startle him into action but just as I was leaning forwards to move the dial Daniel announced the food was ready.

Towards the end of our meal, wholewheat pasta in a peculiar mushroom, sesame and avocado sauce, Daniel asked me about my afternoon. I shrugged and said I'd taken a nap and then gone for a walk, to which Daniel replied I must be getting to know the area well. Pierre shook two tablets out of his medicine bottle and knocked them down with wine, his way, I couldn't help thinking somewhat enviously, of flushing out the day. Once Pierre had merged with the sofa and our dishes were stacked in the sink, the person to wash them still undecided, I felt I'd waited long enough. Just as Daniel was about to get up from the table and head to his desk for a late-night session, I asked about the book.

'Which book?'

'The one with the women,' I said.

'Which?'

'Photographs . . . Of women.'

'Oh, the hysterics.'

'What do you mean?'

Daniel didn't answer.

'Were they agitators?'

'No . . . '

Daniel reached for the dented silver case Pierre had left on the table, extracted a cigarette and lit it, though he rarely smoked.

'Victorian porn?' I thought of Lucian's abundant collection.

He laughed.

'Then what do you mean?'

'No, as I said, they were hysterics.'

'Why do you call them that?'

'I don't. Their doctor did.'

'They all had the same doctor?'

'Yes, they formed part of his collection.'

I couldn't tell whether he was having a laugh.

'Daniel, what are you talking about?'

Lowering his voice a little though Pierre was way past hearing, he began to tell me about a doctor who at the end of the nineteenth century ran the largest neurological clinic in Europe at a hospital in Paris, a former gunpowder factory that was now starting to produce, one could say, a new kind of explosive, and how this doctor called the place his living museum of pathology, with a constantly updated collection.

'And this is the catalogue?'

'I guess you could say that ... he manipulated his patients to pose in different ways to illustrate states of hysteria. And then took pictures.'

His cigarette was more than half ash without him having drawn on it more than twice. He put it out and pushed the saucer to the other side of the table, as if disgusted by it.

'Why do you have this book?'

'Research.'

'They turn you on, don't they?'

'What?'

'You find them attractive.'

I was about to mention the wayward eye at the Drunken Duck when he leaned forwards and asked darkly, 'Marie, what were you doing at my desk?'

'You were out.'

'So?'

'You're always out.'

'That's not true.'

'And when you're home you're with Pierre.'

'He's our guest.'

'No one invited him.'

He threw a glance in Pierre's direction.

'You're welcome to come with us on our walks.'

'I don't want to.'

He shrugged and rose from the table.

'I'm tired, I'll see you tomorrow.'

I said goodnight and remained seated, watching him limp off down the corridor and into his room.

★   ★   ★

Once in bed and fuelled by darkness, my thoughts ran wild as I imagined women pinned down while men gathered round to capture signals and frame their unrest. I thought about this doctor's gaze and how he'd reduced his patients to wraiths, the headboards of their beds like tombstones and the inscriptions on their pillows rewritten. Of female lives condensed into a series of dramatic gestures. The male gaze, nothing seemed free of it. It plundered the living and the dead, manipulating bodies cold and stiff or warm and supple; in either case, depriving them of tranquillity.

I pulled the duvet up around me, half willing Daniel to reappear at the door though I knew that that night he wouldn't, and tried to beckon sleep as I lay with the ghosts of the former couple and the ghosts of the hysterics and the image of our guest stretched out on the sofa, the flat becoming more populated with every passing hour.

12

Given the fog in which he moved, I was surprised when Pierre announced that his last day in Paris was some kind of *Journée du patrimoine*, similar to our National Heritage Day, and suggested we go and see something old and stately. To this day I don't know how he came to choose Challement, a hamlet in Burgundy with a little-known chateau, whether he'd been given a pamphlet or was told by a friend.

We set out at ten and bought three tickets to Clamecy, the station nearest the chateau. Daniel surprised me by coming to sit by my side while Pierre took the seat opposite us. He pulled out a newspaper in German, opened it to the middle and frowned as he began reading something in the upper right-hand corner. Once the train left Paris we rushed through the suburbs and before long were hurtling past wall after wall, or rather one continuous wall, of pine trees, thousands of green needles made one by velocity as they filled our windows. Daniel nodded off, his head resting on a shoulder, but I was eager to stay awake to the scenery.

Every now and then Pierre would reach into his jacket pocket and extract a liquorice coin and slip it into his mouth, making loud smacking noises from behind his newspaper.

After a while the trees fell away, revealing a second landscape hanging parallel to the first: that of the granite sky, which seemed suspended by a few rusted threads that could at any moment snap, leaving this heavy lid to collapse onto the fields and vineyards blanched by winter.

★ ★ ★

Daniel had arranged for a guide. At Clamecy station a man was waiting for us, a tall figure in jeans and a parka slouched against his Renault. He was fluent in English and as he drove us down the country road, rolling up his window as the sky fought for expression, he explained he'd worked in Dover for two years.

Off the main road we turned into a smaller one, then past a copse of trees, up a tiny hill, and towards a large piece of land enclosed by a low crumbling wall. The car came to a halt. We got out, Pierre last, and were led through a gate hanging off its hinges and into a thickly overgrown garden. Its paths were no longer distinct, the original layout blurred by a profusion of dandelions, thistles, nettles and other weeds. There was a brackish pond hemmed in by reeds and flagstone. Grass half a metre high. Overturned bottles and black rubbish bags with dirty rainwater in their dents. The open jaws of a pair of corroded garden scissors. A few metres in the distance, an old car with missing tyres.

From the outside the chateau looked dark and unhappy; rather than a proud survivor, it seemed to resent the fact it had survived.

The air closed in around us as we stepped from the garden into its bare, chilly shambles. During and after the Revolution, our guide explained, most of the building's past had been effaced by both men and erosion, and now little more than its skeleton remained. Yet that skeleton, I saw, was full of character. Over the foot of a stairwell hung a mutilated coat of arms, as if its metal face had received multiple batterings. Between the eighth and eighteenth centuries a string of families — Cizelly, Pioche, du Vierne, La Ferté-Meung and Motte-Dreuzy — had reigned over the seigneury. But with each consecutive owner, our guide added, Challement had fallen into ever more dramatic disrepair and now so little was left, it required a real feat of the imagination to envision the place inhabited by anyone, the rooms so draughty even the ghosts would be blown about.

We climbed a claustrophobic flight of stairs, a segment of the balustrade dangling like a broken arm, and wandered through a set of abandoned rooms. Everywhere I looked, I saw signs of deterioration and decay, of wondrously indifferent dilapidation. Doorways without doors, window frames without panes, deep splintery gashes in the floorboards, gloomy yawning fireplaces, a smashed metal crib. Here and there, the walls and ceiling looked singed and the air smelled faintly of smoke. I pressed my hand against one of the cold walls, the only parts that seemed impervious to time, yet there too I noticed pockmarks in the stone and bits missing from the mortar. Long strands of cobwebs swayed in the corners of the rooms, the absence of windowpanes drawing in currents of cold air from outside. Our guide said it was as if time had stood still in the chateau, but no, on the contrary, everywhere I looked I saw signs of its passage.

At one point I heard the click of a door in another room but there were no doors. At another point, I thought I heard a window slam shut but there were no windows. It must have been the wind.

Back on the ground floor we explored more rooms. Up in the corners I noticed a multitude of nests and wondered whether they belonged to bats or birds who had come to winter inside, though the difference in temperature between indoors and outdoors was minimal. I pulled my coat tightly around me and stuck my hands in the pockets. Daniel had removed his gloves and was writing in his notebook. Pierre stood quietly beside him.

Towards the end of our tour, as we stood in an immense room with high ceilings, once a grand banqueting hall, our guide said, I caught sight of a sooty figure emerging from the fireplace and scurry out of the room. The thing seemed to detach itself from the stone like a shadow fleeing its owner. I cried out. Daniel quickly turned. After a second's delay, Pierre turned too.

The guide asked whether something was the matter. I told him I'd just seen a creature, man or giant rat, I wasn't sure, come out of the chimney.

'Oh, that's our chatelain,' he answered calmly.

'Your chatelain?'

'The owner of the chateau. Half the fee you paid goes to him.'

We wanted to hear more. He hesitated. We clamoured. He hesitated. Daniel said we were soon leaving France, had come all this way, and wanted to depart with something more than what we'd just seen. His words seemed to work.

So, as we stood with our arms huddled into our chests there in the banqueting hall that seemed to grow ever more gusty, we were told the tragic story of Marc Cointe, the chatelain of Challement.

★   ★   ★

Marc Cointe, the man you have just seen, began our guide, was born into the wrong family and the wrong fate. He would have been better suited for just about any other life than the one he was handed. He detested all the trappings on which his family name was embossed yet it was as if the very lines of his life were in the silver before he was even born. As an only child he rode his wooden horse in the meadows and played with the fish and newts in the pond, but by the time he turned fifteen and searched in vain for friends beyond this little kingdom — he had private tutors, no formal schooling — his feelings towards his privileged background began to evolve in complicated ways.

Sadly, nothing was to change. Cointe spent his entire life on the grounds of the chateau, with only two visits to Paris and one to

Provence. Yet he was extremely cultivated, the villagers said, and well read.

But a nihilist.

At his father's funeral he kept his distance, watching from under a tree as the coffin was lowered into the earth by four men, and then drank himself into a stupor in the library. When his mother died a year later, he watched her funeral from a castle window. Both parents were buried in a grove thirty strides from the house but no one ever saw him visit the site.

Cointe had informed opinions on everything — he could hold his own in any debate — but he never wrote anything down. It was enough to share the fruits of his thought with a drunken audience of three: the local farmer, the local welder, and the master of keys of the canal lock.

Until the age of thirty-five, our guide said, the chatelain had liked to entertain. On Friday nights he would invite acquaintances, for they were never true friends, from the village to sample the exquisite vintage wines in his vast cellar, bottles amassed by relatives over the decades. Before long, the contents of his entire *cave* were depleted, and while drinking down the wine, it was said a favourite pastime was to toss eighteenth-century Meissen plates into the air and shoot at them with an antique rifle, shards of porcelain flying asunder. Other family heirlooms met a similar fate.

In those years the chatelain of Challement kept a flock of sheep on the grounds, twelve creatures to which he was famously attached, but one January he slipped into a three-day alcohol coma and when he resurfaced he found them all dead, frozen into different poses, some belly up in the snow with their hooves skywards as if already on their ascent towards animal heaven. He dug a trench, penitently gloveless as he worked, and buried them near his parents.

The years wore on. Marc Cointe grew a beard, stopped washing, and inched closer and closer to *clochard*-dom, our guide continued. His entire inheritance had vanished in drink and nothing remained for the heating or upkeep of the chateau. His cousin, who since childhood had had his sights on the family home, despaired, but there was no legal way of intervening.

The chatelain lost interest in human company. He withdrew from the world and stopped receiving people. Cigarettes, budget wine and round-the-clock fires became his favoured companions. Now wary of everyone, even the master of keys of the canal lock, he rarely answered the door and when he did would be clutching a rusty shotgun. Excursions were limited to weekly visits to the village, where he ran up enormous tabs. The shop owners took pity; some had known him as a child.

Good use was made of all the magnificent fireplaces in the chateau, our guide went on, encouraged by how intently we were listening. The following winter, having already sacrificed two dozen oaks from the estate to make fires, the chatelain began to chop and burn his own furniture. At night the villagers could see steady threads of smoke emerging from the chimneys. After the furniture came the window frames, every door except the main one, and the wood panelling. Then the family portraits. And, finally — he had no choice — the library, until all that was left were a few sacred volumes. Hundreds of books, part of centuries-old collections bound in leather, went up in flames. He had to keep warm.

Over the past few months, the guide said, his descending tone signalling he was nearing the end of his tale, Marc Cointe no longer had a bed (the wood from his four-poster lasted nearly three days) and would sleep inside a mattress in one of the fireplaces. That was where I'd seen him emerge, roused from his slumber, most likely, by our sounds.

I had listened in fascination, and Daniel too, neither of us stirring, oblivious to the cold that penetrated coats and walls.

It was only once the guide finished speaking that we realised Pierre was no longer with us. After a startled exchange of glances the three of us searched the rooms downstairs with a growing sense of alarm. We peered through doorways and windows, tapped the scarred walls as if they might give way to secret passages. Dust reconfigured wherever we went. In the peaceful garden a large magpie had come to perch on one of the bare lindens, but no Pierre. Nor was he in the car. Our guide suggested we try upstairs.

Back up the tight stairwell, this time Daniel leading the way, I grabbed onto the balustrade with a sense of urgency but, feeling it falter, withdrew my grip. I could tell by the near disappearance of his limp that Daniel was starting to panic but fortunately we did not have to look much further, for there in the first large room to the right, the one with the metal crib, stood Pierre face to face with the chatelain.

It was like a scene from a dark children's book. Pierre in his suit with his hair perfectly combed, his expression undisturbed, looking straight at the chatelain, who only a few inches away stared back at him with sunken eyes, his cheeks caved inwards, the hollowness that consumed his face and body scarcely hidden beneath his baggy, rumpled clothes. His coat reached down to the floor; it was impossible to tell whether he wore shoes. An intriguing scar ran down the length of his right cheek, a ruin within a ruin within a ruin.

The noble poet and the noble *clochard*, awake at the same time. Pierre with the ring on his little finger and Cointe with coal-black grime under his long split fingernails. Pierre with his white, clean-shaven, heart-shaped face, a dandelion from the garden emerging from his lapel, opposite the chatelain's angular diamond face, lost in the foliage of his beard. The heart and the diamond, a final hand in a game of cards.

'*Pardonnez-moi?*' Pierre was saying.

'Hic, hic, hic,' said the chatelain.

'*Pardonnez-moi?*' Pierre repeated, leaning forward.

'Hic, hic, hic.'

Pierre produced his cigarette case and held it out. '*Fumez-vous?*'

'Hic, hic, hic,' the chatelain said a third time, and grabbed a cigarette, one more thing to burn.

He shoved it between his lips and was

turning towards the door when he spotted me. To this day I find it hard to describe the look in his eyes as he took in my presence, as if in my face he'd caught a glimpse of someone from his past and was perhaps reliving a moment that struck out from the others. It was an expression of astonishment and nostalgia, of someone faced with a sight he's no longer used to beholding, and he went completely still, staring at me as if he had never seen a woman in his life.

And I couldn't help but stare back, twin currents of excitement and terror braiding through me as I registered his face more closely. His high forehead, marked by pensive grooves, rose proudly away from the cavernous eyes, penetrating in their gloom, and his finely drawn mouth twitched a little at the corners. It was hard to know what to focus on, the combination of his features or on each individually, the same crisis I used to have with paintings. Landscape or detail; in this case, they were equally compelling.

All of a sudden Marc Cointe turned and hurried out of the room, his steps scarcely audible on the stone floor. Without a second thought I ran after him, leaving the others behind. The fugitive black figure moved almost soundlessly, his laboured breathing louder than his steps, a great ball of dust tearing through the darkened rooms of his home, fleeing me and whatever else he might've imagined was chasing him.

I had rarely felt so catalysed, the whole of my being driven by a surge of morbid desire, desperate to be face to face again with this man and see what would happen. And so I pursued him from room to room, through doorways and past walls with cracks, gouges and burns, never losing sight of my target as if my life depended on it, stumbling once over a raised tile but quickly regaining my balance, and when he took a sharp turn round a corner into a small annex containing a narrow tower, I followed.

He was about to start climbing, one foot already on the pitted stair, when I reached out and grabbed the back of his coat. The look of terror when he turned around was horrific, as if I had shattered a hard-won peace and now the entire façade would splinter into a million pieces and scatter on the stone around us. His thin lips were tightly pursed; the cigarette must have dropped out during our chase. The moment I saw his expression I released my grip on his coat, so sooty it had already turned my fingers black, and took a step back, renouncing my pursuit.

Yet before disappearing into the dusk of the tower, the chatelain thrust out an arm, releasing a wave of dust, and scratched my face. One deep scratch with the claws of a frightened cat, yet they weren't claws but long, grimy fingernails that dug into my right cheekbone and dragged their way down. And then he was gone.

Holding a hand up to my stinging cheek and the other in front of me as if clearing a path through the fusty air, I staggered back to the first room, where no one, it seemed, had moved so much as an inch. Pierre was rooted to the same spot where I'd last seen him. He had lit a new cigarette, the rivulet of smoke curling up towards the ceiling. A few feet away stood Daniel, also in the same position as a few minutes earlier, his hands deep in his pockets as if trapped in a thought he couldn't find his way out of.

Someone released the pause button. Daniel freed his hands and his gaze wandered from Pierre to me. It must've been the line of blood down my check, as he did a double take and rushed over.

'What happened?'

'I scraped my face against a wall.'

He frowned and said it looked like a scratch, then pulled a handkerchief from his jacket and pressed it against my broken skin, which made it sting even more. I pushed him away and said I'd be fine.

'But where'd you go?'
'I ran after him.'
'And?'
'Nothing. He disappeared up a turret.'

* * *

The guide was waiting for us in the garden. When and why he'd left the room, nobody knew. In a worn-out voice he called Daniel over to the pond to show him the family of newts that had been living at Challement for centuries.

Pierre, meanwhile, remained near the walls of the chateau. Every now and then I saw him glancing expectantly up at the windows, as if hoping for another encounter with the chatelain. And I too began to glance up, hoping that Marc Cointe would reappear there above like a Green Man carving, branches and foliage snaking out of his mouth, so that I could at least fire off a response with my eyes.

But there was to be no encore.

I felt I had admired a painting, stepped into it, and been cast out. From the looks of it, so did Pierre. For the first time I saw a glimmer of expression pass over his face, a small cloud of unease that moved across his features and dissolved. With the tail end of one cigarette he lit another and turned away, just as Daniel and the guide were returning from the pond.

We drove to the station in uncomfortable silence, Daniel in the front seat beside our guide, neither wearing a seat belt, and I in the back next to Pierre. I was anxious for water and a mirror.

On the platform, a polite *And if you ever come to . . .* farewell. The guide avoided eye contact when shaking my hand and seemed much more concerned with whether my companions had enjoyed their trip. Once on the train, I found the nearest bathroom and inspected my scratch in the mirror. To my surprise it was very thin yet rather deep, like a hairline fissure in a bed of rock. I washed it with soap and water and patted it dry with a rough paper towel. Only after a few minutes of inspection did I realise it was in nearly the same spot as the chatelain's own scar, a long line bisecting his right cheek, starting from below the eye down to somewhere beneath his beard.

★　★　★

That night in bed I must've changed position twenty times, switching from right side to left and then back to right. I got up to open the window and then got up to close it, tried two pillows, then none. Despite these attempts I couldn't rest, my mind captive to one image, hovering there at the centre in great magnification as if an enormous hand kept readjusting the lens: the face of the chatelain. Polished objects reflect the light, unpolished objects trap it.

One thing was clear. I did not feel anger or indignation. I had intruded, he had defended. Every few minutes I'd run my fingers over the scratch that burnt its fine way down my cheek and feel some sort of communion with this chatelain who was at that moment most likely curled up in a shabby mattress in a fireplace, and with a strange flutter I envisioned, how else to put it, the solitude of a man in his architecture.

★   ★   ★

The following morning I rose late to more silence, and an empty flat. A cafetière and two mugs in the sink. The lingering trace of one of Pierre's cigarettes in the air. Three stubs in the saucer. A few more hours, I told myself, only a few more hours.

These hours passed vacantly. Without structure or purpose, my sense of time had weakened. Just as I'd finally motivated myself to get up from the sofa and put on my coat, a heavy rain started to fall, aborting all thoughts of a walk, and I remained indoors watching the curtain of water thick as a double window. Through the parallel panes of glass and water I looked out onto the street, the refracted lights from cars like abrasions in the tarmac, and listened to what sounded like church bells in the distance, as if something greater were trying to assert itself over the weather.

★　★　★

At 4.35 they returned, Daniel carrying an enormous dark blue umbrella that he placed open in the bath to dry. Pierre was wearing a pink flower, possibly from the Luxembourg Gardens, and upon seeing me he plucked it from his lapel and extended it in my direction.

'Did you see the rain?' Daniel asked.

'From indoors,' I said, tucking the flower behind my ear for want of a better idea, then feeling foolish and removing it.

Pierre folded his three suits into his suitcase, emptied the saucer of cigarette stubs into the kitchen bin, and drank a glass of water.

'I'll be back in an hour,' Daniel said, 'I'm taking Pierre to the station.'

'Is he heading back to Stockholm?'

No, Daniel explained, first he would go to Amsterdam to visit a sick friend, a Dutch poet he'd been translating since the seventies, who was now dying of emphysema. From there Pierre would go to Ljubljana to see Gregor and only after that back to Stockholm, where he lived, Daniel added, with his mother in a two-bedroom flat in a sixties tower block.

At the door Pierre extended a hand. 'Nice to see you,' he said. 'Meet you again.'

Daniel picked up the suitcase and Pierre reached for his briefcase. He bowed in my direction, a second more formal farewell. The door clacked behind them.

★   ★   ★

Shortly after they left I spotted Daniel's keys lying on the kitchen table. Caught up in his friend's departure, he had forgotten his set.

I made myself a sandwich and ate it while wandering slowly through the flat, fending off a growing sense of despondency. Once I'd finished eating I was seized by a desire for company, three-dimensional or two, and walked over to Daniel's desk. But the book was no longer there. Hesitantly at first and then more boldly, I searched the drawers, beneath papers and folders, then his room, his suitcase, even lifted the mattress, but the women seemed to have left the premises, retreated into their silent black and white thicket.

Perhaps Daniel had given the book to Pierre, though it scarcely seemed like something that would interest him.

Where had they gone, the women?

⋆　⋆　⋆

Ten, twenty, thirty minutes later — I had no idea — the doorbell rang. A second time. A third. I remained on the sofa, where I'd been sitting, thinking.

Loud knocks, followed by exclamations of a fist that pounded out a phrase, sentence, paragraph.

'Marie, it's me,' his voice reached me as if from a distant peak.

From my position on the sofa facing the entrance, I observed the vibrating wooden rectangle attached to three hinges that separated me from Daniel, and Daniel from the interior of our ephemeral home. Minutes later, a woman's voice. The concierge.

I had no choice. I walked to the door and opened.

He was not smiling.

'I was asleep,' I said.

'And you didn't hear a thing?'

'Nothing.'

The concierge mumbled a few words and started down the stairs. Daniel thanked her, said something about *demain*, and entered the flat.

★　★　★

For our final meal, we returned to the Italian restaurant across the street where we'd gone on our first night. After the waiter had taken our order and brought out bread and olives I thought of asking Daniel what he'd done with the book but refrained; he would know that again I'd trespassed.

We filled the minutes with talk about London, what we would do once we got back, what awaited us where. We spoke, but it was small talk.

Our food arrived quickly.

Daniel sliced his pizza in two with a sharp knife.

'He was quite taken with you, wasn't he, our nobleman?'

'Only at first.'

'Or perhaps it was more you who were taken with him.'

He tore the halves of his pizza apart, then

cut each half into quarters. I reached for my knife and did the same to mine.

'And yours, will you miss him?' I asked.

'Yes, but we'll write.'

'You really disappeared when he was around.'

'Marie, it was a unique opportunity for me. I never meet anyone like him.'

'But that's your choice.'

'Will you miss him too?'

'Pierre? He wasn't much more than a phantom, to be honest.'

'I think he's shy around women.'

'Well, you seemed blind to them when he was here.'

He gave me a quizzical look. 'Meaning?'

'You know what I mean.'

'I thought you'd understand.'

I finished off my wine and refilled the glass.

'Your mood hasn't exactly been jovial,' he added.

'Well, our trip took an odd turn.'

'Trips often do.'

'I guess so.'

'I'm sorry.'

'So, what time does our train leave tomorrow?' I asked.

'Ten fifteen.'

Halfway through dinner a large black spider dropped onto the table — having lowered itself, presumably, from the air vent in the ceiling directly overhead — and scurried across between the dishes, vanishing over the white drop of the tablecloth.

Daniel still had many euros left over and insisted on paying the bill. We traipsed back across the street, through the green doors that felt heavier than ever as I gave them a push, and up to the flat to prepare for our departure. Daniel tackled his desk, returning papers to folders and folders and books to bag, while I packed up my own things, my only purchases during the trip a guidebook, a scarf, some candied chestnuts, and a eucalyptus candle I'd found at a street stall.

It took us no more than an hour, albeit an active one, to divest the flat of our presence. Once we had finished all traces of our visit were withdrawn, our scenes rolled up and waiting by the door. I retired to my room, Daniel to his.

The next morning the concierge rang our bell half an hour earlier than agreed. After a brief march through the flat during which she kept wiping her hands on her apron though I'm sure they weren't wet, she concluded it was in the same state, if not better, than when we arrived, and seemed content with Daniel's tip. Her son, a spindly teenager we'd glimpsed only a few times during our stay, helped carry our bags.

13

The flat smelled as if a dozen cigarettes had been lit, smoked and half put out, the last of them still smouldering in the ashtray. A different kind of cigarette from Pierre's — the odour suggested filterless and hand-rolled. Before even seeing him, I knew Lucian had spent the last few nights in our home.

I was still in the corridor with my bags when he emerged from the kitchen, a cigarette between his lips, a mug of tea in each hand. Upon seeing me he bit down on his cigarette and murmured something, arching his eyebrows in surprise. Seconds later Jane appeared in a black lace negligee. At first I thought it was Lucian's female doppelgänger. Her hair had gone from medium brown to a purple black and was so shiny it looked lacquered, as if the shadows from her face — loneliness, disappointment — had risen and receded into her hair. Over the past weeks, I could see, she had transformed herself into one of Lucian's Goth heroines, Lucretia or Annabel Lee.

'What happened to your cheek?' Jane asked the moment she saw me. The line had been turning a darker crimson as it healed.

'I was scratched by a feral cat.'

She didn't enquire into which cat or where, yet staying on the subject of fauna began telling me about the insect invasion that had taken place in our flat while I was away, a constant hum and buzz, especially at night.

'What sort of insects?'

'Well, mostly moths but also some weird little purplish black ones, I'm not sure what they were.'

'And what did you do with them?'

'I put out loads of strips and even swatted a few.'

I looked around.

'Where are they?'

'Oh Marie, it was disgusting, the strips looked like bristly unshaven legs, I had to throw them out.'

'All of them?'

She rubbed her eyes.

'Yes, I . . . Come, we've just made tea, have some with us.'

I followed her to the kitchen, Lucian doing a U-turn with the mugs.

'Did you get any painting done?'

'Only my room and then the paint ran out,' Jane said, pouring me some tea. 'Maybe next month we can do the rest of the flat together?'

I reached for the jar of honey. Stuck to the inside wall were two cocoons.

'So . . . how was Paris?'

★   ★   ★

When I entered my room and glanced over at the shelf the landscapes looked old, oxidised, depleted, as if over the past two weeks they'd been drained of their vitality. As I drew closer, I saw that most of the moths on them had disintegrated, the crumbling beige of their wings hardly distinguishable from the crumbling beige of their torsos.

At that moment a fly buzzed into sight and perched on the slope of the mountaintop, crawled a few paces, then moved onto the volcano, where it briefly circled the red crater before flying off.

I picked up an eggshell, the one with the tiny door into night, and held the doorknob between my thumb and forefinger and pulled. For the first time ever it seemed to resist so I pulled harder. All of a sudden the door was in my hand, a rectangular gash out of which night could come spilling out, yet when I peered in I saw only dull black dabbed with spots from a silver metallic marker.

Next I picked up the autumn eggshell and brought it close to the lamp. I could only

229

focus on the clumps of glue that fastened the rough paper leaves to matchsticks. When I turned to the mountain and volcano they too seemed like something pawed at with impatience by a child. They had never appeared so crude, nothing more than coarse dioramas by an amateur, and the more I stood back and stared the more I felt the landscapes vanishing before my eyes.

★ ★ ★

But maybe all landscapes vanish after a while or one just comes to prefer others. My great-grandfather's final years were lived out in a cottage at the bottom of a field in Yorkshire. For days on end he wouldn't exchange a word with anyone; the silence of low ceilings and unclipped hedges was more appealing than any human voice, he said, and his eyes had taken in enough faces to fill three lifetimes.

Only after my trip to Paris could I understand the weariness he once described as he was nearing the end of his time at the Gallery. After forty-six years there who could blame him, but even I, after a mere decade, felt pangs of disenchantment, my feet growing heavy as I climbed the steps to the staff entrance the following Monday. At first I was so indifferent to everything around me I almost forgot to check the plaque to see whether any names had been added while I was away but, needless to say, nothing eventful had taken place in my absence. When I put on my uniform the greyness spilled over my insides too, pressing down on my chest and ribs, cancelling out all colour. My tie kept coming out crooked, as if in two weeks I'd forgotten how to knot it, and I had to ask a colleague for help. At least I was assigned the Sainsbury Wing that day, I would've sunk into mortal tedium with the Impressionists, but even the gilt on the medieval panels and paintings refused to shine and not a single saint beamed himself out to distract me. At lunch I had no desire to tell Roland about Paris, though he bombarded me with questions and was more animated than usual, clenching his jaw with a mania I'd never seen before.

* * *

All around London the trees remained stripped by winter, their bare branches like bouquets of burnt sparklers. In the sky charcoal clouds hitched rides on strong currents of wind. Strange face-like patterns appeared in the cracked ice of the pavements,

231

rising up from the ground like tombstone rubbings. Things appeared and disappeared, and the scratch on my face had just about healed, now a thin, pinkish line down the length of my cheek.

★ ★ ★

Daniel, meanwhile, seemed to be flourishing. We had yet to meet up since Paris but had spoken on the phone. From the moment he returned, he'd been gripped by writing fever. He'd walked into his flat, thrown a sheet over the wooden contraption, and sat down by the nautilus shell at his desk. He sent out his poems and wrote more and more new ones. With less patience than usual, I listened on as he told me how for years he'd been inching towards the haiku, circling the form and making small advances, and had now finally started the process, he said, *a miniaturisation of existence*. But they were urban haikus rather than hymns to nature. Roaches instead of grasshoppers, pigeons instead of swallows, pavements instead of riverbanks, television towers instead of trees. His correspondents had cautioned him from falling into the haiku trap. Few things were more tempting, they knew, than to pare down life and apply X-ray vision to each day, but one had to be careful; the form was deceptively simple.

* * *

Two weeks after our trip I was standing in the threshold of Rooms 65 and 66, with just a little more presence in Room 65 since it contained a showcase with one of our very few Dürers, an oil panel on pearwood, St Jerome on one side and on the other a comet, the man in his wilderness and a yellow flash with a red tail bursting out from dark clouds in a night sky, when Daniel appeared. He seemed to have been in a hurry, hair matted to forehead and scarf nearly trailing the floor, but he slowed down once he spotted me, and stopped to catch his breath.

'Hello.' I moved towards him. 'Is everything okay?'

The red of his face retreated slowly, replaced by winter white.

Without answering he removed his gloves, reached into his pocket and pulled out a crumpled newspaper clipping.

'Thought you might like to see what just arrived in the post, courtesy of Pierre.'

I unfolded what appeared to be an obituary from a French newspaper, dated four days earlier. In the upper left-hand corner was a photograph of a striking man with large eyes and shoulder-length hair. Just as I was starting to see the resemblance, Daniel began to translate, lowering his voice as three new visitors entered the room and came to stand at a painting nearby. Normally I would have asked him to wait until they'd left, but at that moment impatience was burning a path straight through me.

In recent days, the region's official chronicler had written, the chatelain had gone to live in his car and from his car it was a brief journey, without any need for petrol or accelerator, to the grave. He might have died overnight or perhaps in the morning; he wasn't found till the afternoon, by a former gardener who had come to tow away an abandoned tractor now home to a family of foxes and had noticed a leg hanging out of the 1976 Ford GS. Drawing closer, he saw the rest of the body in the back seat. The chatelain's eyes were concave, his skin a pale green. A tiny spider, the last sign of life, crawled out of his beard.

At the top of the clipping Pierre had written, *Il quitta le réel.*

'Meaning what?' I asked.

Daniel shrugged. 'He quit the real.'

I felt as if the floor of Room 65 were being seized by the corners and tilted sharply to the left, my legs about to buckle under. I looked around for a seat but that day, inexplicably, there was no chair nearby. Daniel studied my face and I studied his. I realised I had no sense of his feelings regarding the chatelain. He lingered another moment, then folded the clipping and returned it to his pocket. A fresh batch of visitors entered the room. He turned to me and said, *Goodbye, let's speak later*, whispering the words so quickly they sounded like a foreign language. And that was it. He walked out and left me alone with the newsflash.

All I could think of as I stood there was the man entombed in his car, his leg hanging out and the spider in his beard, and above that image, disturbing enough on its own, was the awful thought, circling like a crow overhead, that in some way I had hastened his death by disturbing him. Why else would he have gone from sleeping in his chimney to his car? I struggled to remain composed in front of the visitors but began to feel increasingly dizzy. The cold sandstone of the wall I was leaning against seemed to soften under the pressure of my hand. I looked into the centre of the room and started to imagine that the Dürer panel would at any moment burst open and release the comet from the parabola in which it had been fixed, nebulous matter spilling out into the halls of the Gallery, a new incident in cometary history to mark the news we'd just heard. Yet, like so much else, it wasn't to happen, and before long I moved on to Room 67.

* * *

Jane was out when I returned to the flat, which was just as well though by then nothing would have stopped me. Without taking off my coat I headed to my room and over to the shelf and one by one picked up my landscapes. I grabbed them from their peaks or foundations, whichever was first to touch my fingers, and began. I held the volcano from its base and pushed upwards, trying to force the so-called magma up through the mantles of crust and into the crater, but the whole thing just collapsed in my hand. I scratched at the mountainside, bits of slope getting stuck under my fingernails, including the moth. It was harder to destroy the cliffs of Pegwell Bay, no matter the angle the plywood wouldn't give, but I tore off as much as I could from the top and shredded the gold leaf into jagged rays. With the seascapes I broke off the waves of crystallised sugar, amazed by how much they'd hardened, then tore at the dark cotton clouds and broke the masts in two. Every matchstick that had transformed into a tree went back to being a matchstick, albeit no longer whole. The yielding of the eggshells was especially satisfying, little domed worlds that crushed at the centre of my palm, and the more I thought back on the chatelain the greater my contempt for these misshapen things.

First in my hand and then under my foot, I demolished each one, listening to the symphony of cracking, crumbling and caving in. As if a thousand papery wings were guiding my movements, the crushed moths adding a silvery dust, I tore up paper skies, uprooted little trees and crumpled aluminium lakes, destroying landscapes I knew I was never going to inhabit, *in case of tempest this garden will close*, and I didn't pause for a second until I'd annihilated every one, for in the end we are all either gatekeepers or trespassers, and I knew I would never want to have to choose between the two.

⋆ ⋆ ⋆

As soon as I opened my eyes the next morning I looked over at the area beneath the shelf. Tiny bits of eggshell lay strewn across the floor like in one of those Dutch paintings. I left them there for two days before sweeping everything up with a small dustpan and brush, the crushed white clinging to the small dustballs that had formed. All the detritus, the broken matchsticks, the torn paper, the shreds of cotton, looked like nothing more than the aftermath of a children's party. And though I searched for it, would have even held on to it as some kind of talisman, I never found the cat's tooth once it separated from the grotto where it had lived for over fifteen years.

★ ★ ★

The person I needed to speak to at Human Resources was flipping through a catalogue when I went down to see her during my first tea break.

'Hi Marie, what can I do for you?'

She closed the catalogue and smiled wearily.

'I want to hand in my notice.'

The words came out more naturally than I'd expected. From the corner of my eye I saw the others look up from their desks. Such drab surroundings down there, below all the splendour, I wondered whether they cared.

'You want to leave the Gallery?'

'Yes . . . '

I looked straight into her eyes, drawing myself up to my full height.

'Would you like to take a seat?'

'No, thank you.'

'Okay . . . ' she trailed, 'you've been here for quite a long time, haven't you?' She swivelled round in her chair and opened the top drawer of a filing cabinet behind her, from which she extracted a thick folder. Flip flip flip till my name came up.

'Yes,' she fingered the papers, 'nearly ten years . . . '

'The boredom gets to you eventually, doesn't it?' someone said from his desk. The others laughed.

'No, it's not that.'

'Is there a problem, Marie? Something we can help you with?' she asked in a conciliatory tone.

'No.'

She stared fixedly to see whether I was telling the truth. I lowered my eyes.

'There's really nothing wrong?'

'Nothing.'

'Well then how soon would you like to leave us?'

'Whenever the contract runs out.'

She nodded.

'There's a waiting list, you know, for a job

like yours. If the list were a queue, it would wrap itself all the way round the building. Are you sure you don't want to think it over?'

'Yes, I'm sure.'

'Very well, then. Your notice period is four weeks. After that, you're free to do whatever you wish.'

*   *   *

When I told him my plans at lunch, though the only concrete one was to leave the Gallery, Roland lay down his fork, reached for his water and began sipping at it compulsively. And what next, he asked, to which I had no answer. New subjects, I told him, and new verbs. I had no idea what those would involve, I admitted, but my days would have something like a new vocabulary. No more standing back and watching over culture. I still had four weeks left but in a symbolic act towards the end of lunch we exchanged numbers, for the first time ever, I realised, and agreed to meet for drinks at least once a month, the sort of promise one sincerely means while already doubting it will be fulfilled.

*   *   *

Jane's concern was how I was going to pay the rent. I reassured her I would begin trawling various job listings that weekend and start making phone calls. The Gallery would write me a reference letter and there was no reason why it shouldn't be good. And I had a tiny bit of savings, enough to last a month or two, by which time I'd surely have found a new job. The world felt large again, almost infinite, and I wanted to postpone the moment till I committed to new walls and rules.

At first Daniel was sceptical, frowning as he listened to my decision, but after a few days he rang up and gave his support and even confessed to sometimes having wondered whether like my great-grandfather I would turn grey and hunched in the rooms of the Gallery, a fate I often thought I'd share with him.

⋆ ⋆ ⋆

After the destruction of my objects it took weeks to accustom myself to their absence. Each time I entered my room I'd look over at the empty shelf expecting to see them, the way you glance at the same spot on the wall where you once found a large spider, half hoping, half dreading, to see it

241

there again although you removed it with a glass and paper long ago. One evening I finally moved an armful of paperbacks to the shelf and propped them up with tea tins full of gravel and, with that, the imprint was gone.

★ ★ ★

In bed at night, and during lulls at the Gallery, the chatelain would come lurching into my thoughts. Sometimes I could see his face, but often it was only the back of him or that first glimpse from afar, a human-size clump of ashes blown out of the fireplace. Over the weeks he began to feel about as real as Daniel's Hungarian hypnotist, and I wondered whether this would end up being the story I'd carry round and sometimes unfold from my pocket. Marc Cointe quit the real, Pierre had said, but maybe he'd never belonged to it. Each time I doubted I'd pull out the evidence and lay it on the table: four witnesses, a printed obituary with a photograph, and, not least, the scar on my cheek, now a groove so pale I had to tilt my head under a bright light to locate it in the mirror. All real.

★ ★ ★

Late one afternoon a young sketcher entered my room at the Gallery with his notebook. Dark hair in a ponytail, always the same beige vest and scuffed suede boots. I'd seen him many times before. He sat down on the bench and began sketching Giovanni Bellini's *Madonna of the Meadow* so feverishly he seemed to forget everything but himself and the painting. I strained to get a better view but my seat was too far away. He was working with such intensity, my curiosity grew and grew, and I finally got up and walked around, pretending to check something behind him, and was more than a little surprised when I glanced down and saw that instead of a sweet infant Christ the Madonna was holding a foetus with enormous eyes and frog-like hands, its fingertips like suction cups and toothed circular mouth a red sea anemone that seemed to move on the page. Given his docile manner I'd always assumed the young sketcher was producing elegant, faithful copies of the works in our Gallery, not mangling them. The Madonna — beautifully rendered, he was an excellent draughtsman — was cradling a baby Jesus from outer space.

Four weeks passed in a gust.

★ ★ ★

At the start of my final day, not wanting to rush, I set out for work half an hour early. 'There are beggars and buskers on this train. Please do not encourage their presence by supporting them,' said the announcement on the Tube, but that morning I encouraged them with small coins, those tiny acts of generosity you're prone to when feeling, however briefly, that the universe is finally on your side.

★   ★   ★

As I stood in the threshold of 45 and 46 watching strangers fill the rooms, my head began to swarm with images from the past and present, like in those old paintings or, more often, panels, with continuous narrative, in which different scenes or chapters of a saint's life crowd the same space with little perspective, and I thought back on my years at the Gallery, the thousands of hours spent standing and sitting, watching over immobile images and mobile figures, and I wondered what I would miss. It had been a second home, this geometry of square rooms, rectangular halls, circular junctions between quadrilaterals, the links, axes and extensions, the vestibules and sub-vestibules ... But apart from Roland and the St Jeromes, it was hard to tell what else might return in dreams; only later would I know.

★   ★   ★

At 6.10 in the changing room, I began saying farewell to my uniform. I removed my jacket and laid it on the bench, brushing off two strands of hair from the collar. I undid the button and zip and stepped out of my trousers, taking time to pull each leg out. Then came the seven buttonholes down my chest, which I tackled as slowly as I could. Once freed from the lilac blouse, I folded it neatly and also laid it on the bench though I knew everything would soon be tossed into the wash. I was sad to give up the purple tie but knew I'd never wear it in the real world.

The museum stayed open three hours later on Fridays but unless we regulars worked overtime, our shift would end at the usual hour and part-timers would come in and take over from six to nine, a comfortable relay though I'd miss hearing Henry's jangling of keys, and it always threw me off a little to see unknown faces in the changing rooms as I was getting ready to leave.

That evening I didn't head out once I had put on my civvies. Instead of making my way to the exit as I normally did, I returned to the second floor in my black wool skirt and high boots, ones I'd treated myself to the week before to mark the end of an era, and crossed section after section of my former kingdom, past men and women in grey, many of whom I didn't recognise, past paintings whose shapes and colours I registered out of the corner of my eye, and kept walking until I reached Room 30.

Two men, Spaniards I think, were standing in front of her speaking loudly and gesturing. One of them moved his hand across the air as if following the contours of her body, the slope of her shoulder and the dip at her waist, while the other nodded in agreement and then repeated the movement. I waited until they had walked off.

It had been a while since we'd been face to face. I drew near for a close look. I was struck by how calm she appeared, at such peace in her salmon-pink boudoir, so oblivious to the strong emotions she'd stirred up in men and women over the years, and wondered whether if I stood there long enough some of this dignified calm would seep into me. I could almost feel the warmth of her enclosure, the brush of silks and satins, the sound of her breath as she gazed into the mirror Cupid held up. I'd rarely, if ever, seen such a beautiful body, a smooth and perfect arabesque, the kind any woman would dream of having.

As I stood there I noted a detail not in the paint layer but in the painting, something guides would often mention, the fact that the face in the mirror and the pearly woman outside didn't match up, a disjunct between the reflection and the reflected. The face in the mirror was rounder and swarthier, one could see, out of focus and hard to read, while the face outside, at least judging from the one-quarter profile, seemed to belong to someone paler, more delicate and ideal. Light outside, shadow in the mirror, perfection beyond, something rougher in the reflected.

I took a few steps back and sat down on the leather sofa facing the painting. Yes, I could still see the dissonance, and for the first time it bothered me. I stood up again and returned to the painting, leaning further in to inspect the face in the mirror once more, but now instead of Venus's blurred features another face appeared, that of a pale woman with a jagged black fringe and longish nose, her eyes searching and intense, and I blinked a few times to make sure I wasn't imagining things, but no, for a few seconds a very familiar face gazed back out at me, and I wondered whether Mary Richardson too had caught a quick glimpse of herself in this mirror.

'Excuse me, Miss . . . Excuse me?'

I turned towards the voice. It belonged to a young woman in uniform, with greyish eyes and six or seven silver hoop earrings climbing up her ear.

'Could you step back a little, please?'

I obeyed.

'A little more?'

A mechanical second step.

Satisfied, she returned to her post. I turned back to the painting but the spell had been broken. I moved on from Venus and pretended to study another Velázquez on her left but had no interest just then in Philip IV and decided it was time to leave.

With steps so slow I could hear the creaking leather of my boots, I made my way towards one of the exits and out of Room 30, then crossed the Sunley Room and the Central Hall, into the main vestibule across its mosaic floor and then down the stairs, past the shop on the right, and down one more flight and out into the cool wintry air of the portico where people stood with cigarettes taking in the view of the square. Once past the eight Corinthian columns I took a deep breath, released, forever, from the museum's clench of hours, released, now and always, from both collections, and picking up speed I rushed headlong down the steps like a child, five, ten, fifteen steps in a new direction, and wasn't bothered by the backs of statues below for they would no longer be my daily view, and I wondered which way to walk, whether home or to Soho.

While I tried to make up my mind, I stopped to watch a pavement artist, a young man who sometimes came and unfurled his copy of *The Last Supper* outside the Gallery and anchored it with four stones, touching up his canvas until the winter light withdrew, and he usually stayed on for a few more hours since I'd see him again after work, and that evening I stood and watched him kneeling beneath the glow of the street lamps as he counted out the change in his cap, people hurrying past in the evening chill, some stepping on the corners, even on the faces, of his work, which as far as I could tell was a very accomplished replica in oil paint of the original, but the young man didn't seem to mind, even when a man in furs stepped right on Christ's face with his large black shoe or when a pigeon began pecking at Judas Iscariot, and once he'd finished counting his coins he dropped them into a leather pouch which he tucked into his jacket and then placed his cap back on his head, and, still on his knees, lifted each stone from the corners of his scroll, piled them to one side, dusted off the painting's surface with the back of his hand, and began to carefully roll it up, the long table and the apostles gradually disappearing into shadow. From a few feet away I continued to watch, not stirring until he had finished rolling his canvas into a large, heavy cylinder he then tucked under his arm though it seemed far too unwieldy, and, with confident steps, headed back into the tumult of the city.

Acknowledgements

Thank you first and foremost to Parisa Ebrahimi, my extraordinary editor at Chatto & Windus. And to Lauren Wein, Andrew Kidd, Anna Stein, Suzanne Dean, Poppy Hampson and Sally Riley.

Thank you to the following friends: Devorah Baum, Mathilde Bonnefoy, Michael Bucknell, Rubén Gallo, Astrid Gessert, Terence Gower, Phillipa Horan, Mary Horlock, Nicole Krauss, Klaus Kropfinger & Helga von Kügelgen, Darian Leader, Wolfe Lenkiewicz, Neil Porter, Simon Preston, Sally Read, Lorna Scott Fox, Irene Skolnick, Josh Appignanesi.

And in memory of Malcolm Bowie.

Thank you to Ledig House, the MacDowell Colony and Santa Maddalena Foundation residencies.

Thank you to the Fondo Nacional para la Cultura y las Artes.

Thank you to Nicholas Donaldson at the National Gallery archives and to art conservator Christian Scheidemann for sharing his knowledge of craquelure.

Thank you to the kind guards at the

National Gallery who patiently answered my questions.

And thank you, immensely and forever, to my parents and Eva.

I am particularly indebted to the following sources: George Dangerfield's *The Strange Death of Liberal England*, Dario Gamboni's *The Destruction of Art: Iconoclasm and Vandalism since the French Revolution*, Knut Nicolaus's *The Restoration of Paintings*, and Mary Richardson's *Laugh a Defiance*.

We do hope that you have enjoyed reading this large print book.

Did you know that all of our titles are available for purchase?

We publish a wide range of high quality large print books including:
Romances, Mysteries, Classics
General Fiction
Non Fiction and Westerns

Special interest titles available in large print are:
The Little Oxford Dictionary
Music Book
Song Book
Hymn Book
Service Book

Also available from us courtesy of Oxford University Press:
Young Readers' Dictionary
(large print edition)
Young Readers' Thesaurus
(large print edition)

For further information or a free brochure, please contact us at:
Ulverscroft Large Print Books Ltd.,
The Green, Bradgate Road, Anstey,
Leicester, LE7 7FU, England.
Tel: (00 44) **0116 236 4325**
Fax: (00 44) **0116 234 0205**

THE LOVE AFFAIRS OF NATHANIEL P.

Adelle Waldman

Nathaniel Piven is a rising star in Brooklyn's literary scene. After an early life as a class-A nerd and several lean, striving years, he now (to his surprise) has a lucrative book deal, his pick of plum magazine assignments, and the attentions of many desirable women: Juliet, the hotshot business journalist; Elisa, Nate's gorgeous ex-girlfriend, now friend; Hannah, lively, fun and 'almost universally regarded as nice and smart, or smart and nice'. Within this twenty-first century literary conclave, wit and conversation are not all dead. But is romance?

AN ENGLISHWOMAN IN NEW YORK

Anne-Marie Casey

When Lucy's husband loses his job and is relocated to New York, she is forced to give up her posh London life and move to a tiny Manhattan apartment. Homesick and resentful at first, Lucy soon finds herself embarking on an exhilarating new affair — no, not with her husband (although she is surprised to find they do still love each other), but with the city itself and the three women she meets at the school gates who, against all odds, become her friends . . .

THE SECRET OF ELLA AND MICHA

Jessica Sorensen

Ella and Micha have been best friends since childhood, until one tragic night shatters their relationship and Ella decides to leave everything behind, including Micha, to start a new life at college. But now it's summer break and Ella fears everything she worked so hard to bury might resurface, especially with Micha living right next door. Micha is sexy, smart, confident, and can get under Ella's skin like no one else can. And he's determined to win back the girl he lost, no matter what it takes.